Does it have to be Princess?" Danny pleaded. "You got to pick the dog; shouldn't we get to pick her name?"

"No way!" I said. I know my brothers.

"Kickball," suggested Miguel.

"Twinkletoes," suggested Danny.

"Señorita Fancypants!"

"Lady Snooty McSnooterfluff of the Waterford McSnooterfluffs!"

"Stop it!" I said. "Her name is Princess!"

"Her eyes look like little black buttons," Miguel said.

"Buttons!" Danny cried. The puppy leaped to her paws and scrambled onto Danny's lap. "See, she likes it."

At least it was better than Lady McSnooterfluff or Kickball. But what about my perfect little Princess?

Get into some

Pet Trouble

Runaway Retriever

Loudest Beagle on the Block

Mud-Puddle Poodle

Bulldog Won't Budge

Pet Trouble

Mud-Puddle Poodle

by T. T. SUTHERLAND

SCHOLASTIC INC.
New York Toronto London Auckland Sydney
Mexico City New Delhi Hong Kong Buenos Aires

ISBN-13: 978-0-545-10243-8
ISBN-10: 0-545-10243-X

12 11 10 9 8 7 6 5 4 3 2   9 10 11 12 13 14/0

Printed in the U.S.A.
First printing, July 2009

For Sunshine, my own Buttons ☺

CHAPTER 1

When my mom said we could (*finally*) get a dog, I knew exactly what I wanted.

But you won't understand it until you know a little about me, so that's where I'm going to start.

My name is Rosie Sanchez. I have curly black hair and brown eyes and my favorite color is pink. I'm ten years old. And I have four older brothers.

Four.

Four older brothers.

Try to imagine that. I'll help: For starters, they are loud. They are dirty. They crash around the house breaking things and making as much noise as a herd of hippos all day long.

And they never pay any attention to *me*, because I'm "too little," even though Danny is only one year older than me and I think it is not fair at all.

So why would I want a dog like that? Another big, loud, dirty animal in the house — we already have four!

No sir. I knew what I wanted. I wanted a little girl dog with pink ribbons in her hair like mine. She would be sweet and quiet and pretty and ladylike, just like me.

Well, OK. I'm not always sweet. Or quiet. Fine, or ladylike! But can you blame me? Just think about what I have to compete with! If I'm going to get anywhere in this house, I have to make a lot of noise, too.

But once I had my perfect dog, I knew everything would be different. She would be *my* dog. She'd help balance out all the boy-boy-boy rumpus going on in my house all the time. She would be my little princess, and then we could ignore my brothers together, the way they always ignore me.

Well, things didn't turn out quite the way I planned. . . .

Danny was the one who started it. His best friend, Parker, got a dog right before school started, and Danny *would not shut up* about that dog for, like, two weeks straight. It was "Guess what Merlin did," and "Merlin's such a great dog," and "It'd be so awesome if Merlin had a friend, ahem ahem," and on and on and *on*.

We all finally got to meet this miracle dog on the Thursday before the talent show, when Parker brought him over. I will admit, Merlin was really pretty. His fur was shiny and golden and he had this sweet, smiley face. But after he left, our nice blue couch was *covered* in golden dog fur. My brothers didn't care, but I did! I like things to be neat and clean. No big sweaty brothers are allowed in my room, so it's by far the cleanest room in the house.

After Parker and Merlin left, Danny gave Mom this begging look. He made his eyes really big and clasped his hands together under his chin.

"*Please*, Mom," he said. "Please please *please* can we get a dog?"

He didn't know I was listening. I was hiding behind the couch (the now extremely furry couch) because I *knew*, I just *knew* he was going to try this trick.

"Well . . ." Mom said. "He *is* a really sweet dog, isn't he?"

"If we got another golden retriever," Danny said, "then he could play with Merlin! It would be awesome!"

"Oh, no you don't!" I yelled, popping out from behind the couch. Danny jumped a mile, which was totally hilarious. I wagged my finger at him. "You know I don't want a golden retriever, Danny! *I* should get to decide what kind of dog we get, because I'm the youngest, so I'll be home with her after you're all in college!"

"Only one year longer than me!" Danny shouted. "And that's only if we don't throw you out sooner for being bossy and spying on us all the time!"

"You were being sneaky!" I hollered.

"*You* are being a *pain in the butt*!" Danny hollered back.

"I'm going to go lie down," Mom said.

"See, look, you ruined it!" Danny yelled at me. "Mom, wait!"

"All right, listen," Mom said. "We can get a dog. But you five have to agree on what kind to get. That's the deal." Then she went to put her earplugs in, which happens a lot.

She should have known that "deal" wouldn't work in our house, though. My brothers and I never agree on *anything*.

When we went to New York City on vacation last year, Danny wanted to go to Yankee Stadium, Carlos wanted to go to the Museum of Natural History to see the dinosaur bones, Miguel wanted to go to Rockefeller Center and look for celebrities, and Oliver wanted to visit NYU, because that's where he wants to go to college.

I wanted to go to American Girl Place and have tea at the Plaza just like Eloise, my favorite book character.

You see why I have to be really loud to get anything I want?

In the end Mom took me to the Plaza while Dad took all my brothers to Yankee Stadium, which was fine by me.

But it wasn't going to be that easy to solve *this* argument, unless we got *five* dogs, which I didn't think Mom (or our furniture) was entirely ready for.

The big fight happened a couple of days later, when we were all sitting around the dinner table on Saturday, the night after the talent show. Even Oliver was there, which was amazing. He's seventeen, so on Saturdays he's usually out with his girlfriend, Miru. My mom says Miru is "*muy bonita*" and I say she is way way way too cool for Oliver.

Anyway, I think he stuck around this Saturday night because we'd all been fighting all day about what kind of dog to get. He probably knew that if he left he would definitely lose.

It was Dad's turn to cook, so we were having his famous chili con carne, which I like because it tastes good but I don't like because it's messy and if I get any on my clothes it's impossible to get out. Plus the boys always spill it all over the pretty yellow tablecloth because, if I haven't mentioned this already, *they are slobs*.

"So," Dad said when we were almost done eating, "I hear we're talking about dogs."

Poor Dad. He's a big-shot lawyer, so he works all the time, and when he's really busy he gets totally spaced-out like he can't think about anything but his cases. And then when he comes back down to earth he's weeks behind on everything that's happening. He always notices my haircut about ten days after I get one. He'll ask Danny questions about baseball in the winter and soccer in the spring, even if he's just been to one of his games that week. Last year he congratulated Carlos (my third-oldest brother) on winning the seventh-grade science fair — seriously, no kidding — a *month* after it happened. I think he still hasn't noticed that Oliver finally has a girlfriend.

So he had no idea what kind of fireworks he was setting off with that question. Mom did, though. She flinched as soon as the words were out of his mouth.

"Everyone is being unfair!" Danny shouted immediately. "It was *my* idea to get a dog! I want a golden retriever!"

"What? I've *always* wanted a dog!" Miguel cried. He's fifteen and he's turned into Mr. Cool ever since he got to high school. I swear he uses more hair gel than the entire cast of Mom's favorite *telenovela*. "Mom, remember, I asked for a dog years and years ago, before you could even *talk*, Danny! And I want a Rottweiler!"

"No way!" Carlos chimed in. "We should get a Border collie! Border collies are *sooo* smart!"

Danny rolled his eyes. Of course Carlos wanted a smart dog. He's worlds smarter than the rest of us. I could just imagine Carlos and a Border collie solving calculus problems together and laughing at the rest of the eighth-graders.

"We *have* to get a giant schnauzer," Oliver announced firmly. He always tries to sound like being oldest means he gets to make the decisions, but it never works.

"I don't know what that is," Danny said, "but it sounds like a cookie, not a dog. Lame! Golden retriever!"

I banged my fork on the table (checking first to make sure there was no chili on it). "No, no, no!" I yelled. "None of these big dogs! I WANT A TOY POODLE!"

My brothers all groaned loudly. Danny pretended to thump his head on the table in despair. Of course, he got chili in his hair, but I wasn't about to tell him that.

"Absolutely not," Oliver said.

"A small *girly* dog!" Miguel whined. "No way!"

"The guys would laugh at me *so much* if we got a little fluffy dog," Danny protested.

"Mom, tell her no," Carlos said.

"Shut up!" I yelled. "I can have an opinion! I WANT A TOY POODLE!"

"This has been going on for three days," Mom said to Dad.

"Oh, dear," Dad said, rubbing his head.

I thought about shouting "I want a toy poodle" again, but Dad looked like he was thinking, so I decided not to. My friends think my house is total chaos, but I've mostly figured out when it's the right time to shout and when it's the right time to be quiet. When Dad has that little frown on his face, I know he's about to say something clever. And if I am quiet right then, most of the time he'll think I'm the one being good, and he'll let me win.

"We can figure this out," he said. "Everyone stay here." He jumped up and went into the basement, which is where he works when he's home.

Danny scowled at me across the table. I poked my tongue out at him.

"Seriously, you guys," Oliver said in this *OK-now-let's-be-grown-ups* voice. "We really have to get a giant schnauzer. It's one of the only breeds Miru isn't allergic to."

"Poodles are hy-po-all-er-gen-ic, too," I said. I had spent *hours* memorizing that word. It means they don't shed and so most people aren't allergic to them. It's one of the best things about poodles. I knew Mom would like that, too, because she'd probably be the one vacuuming up all the dog hair if we got a big shedding dog.

"Yeah, but poodles are stupid," Carlos said.

"Carlos," Mom said warningly.

"*Actually*, they're the second-smartest of all the dog breeds," I said. "It's true. You can look it up on the Internet." Yeah, I said it snottily. He deserved it. He thought he was so brilliant, but he didn't really know anything about poodles.

"Yeah, right," Danny said. "Like anything with a head that small could possibly have a brain."

"They're smarter than *you* are!" I flared.

"*Rosie,*" Mom said.

I was pretty close to flinging a spoonful of chili at Danny — I didn't even care that it would make a mess — but luckily just then Dad came clumping back up the stairs. He was carrying the whiteboard from above his desk, which he had erased completely. It was such a strange sight that we all shut up for about thirty seconds, just staring at him.

"Please join me in the living room," Dad said with a grin.

We all shot out of our chairs and stampeded into the living room like rampaging water buffalo. Listen, I *want* to be ladylike, but if you don't move fast in this house, you end up sitting on the floor. I made it to the big green flowery armchair before Danny did, which made him even madder. But he still beat Carlos to the couch, so it was my genius thirteen-year-old brother who ended up sitting on the carpet.

Dad balanced the whiteboard on a chair from the kitchen and drew a chart on it that looked like this:

Name	Breed	Round 1	Round 2	Round 3	Winner
ROSIE	toy poodle				
DANNY	golden retriever				
CARLOS	Border collie				
MIGUEL	Rottweiler				
OLIVER	giant schnauzer				

"Did I get that right?" Dad asked. "Are those the breeds you all have decided on?"

"Toy poodle, toy poodle!" I shouted.

"Yeah, Dad, that's right," Carlos said.

"Woo! Rottweiler!" Miguel yelled.

"No — woo, golden retriever!" Danny hollered.

"Dad, what does the rest of it mean?" Oliver asked. "Round one? Round two?"

Dad smiled. "We're going to decide this fairly. We're going to play a game."

CHAPTER 2

I was instantly suspicious. As you can imagine, it's hard to win games in my house when there are four big older brutes competing against me.

"There better not be running involved," I said. "Or baseballs. Or eating." We discovered last summer that Danny can eat twelve hot dogs in a row without throwing up. *Thirteen* hot dogs, not so much.

Dad shook his head. "Don't worry, Rosie. We're trying to be fair here. So, since you all are *so* sure of the breeds you want — we're going to find out how much you know about them."

I seriously nearly punched the air, I was so excited. Nobody knew this, but I'd been thinking about poodles for months. I'd read everything I could find about them on the Internet. My brothers thought I only wanted one because they're little and princessy-looking, which was kind of true, but there are lots of little princessy-looking dogs and I had studied them all before deciding on a toy poodle. Definitely a toy poodle.

"Señora, if I could request your assistance," Dad said gallantly to Mom. He whispered to her and she went into the study and came back with a sheet of blank paper and a pencil for each of us. "We can begin . . . Round one!"

I took the pencil from Mom and grabbed a big art book of Aztec monuments from the coffee table to balance the paper on.

"Lady and gentlemen!" Dad said. He clasped his hands behind his back and walked up and down. I could tell he was pretending to be in court. I saw him present a case to a jury once. He's really convincing.

Someday I'd like to win arguments like he does, by knowing stuff and saying it right, but that's not how they're won in my house, so for now I have to stick to being as loud as possible.

"Your first task," Dad said, "is . . . to *draw* the kind of dog you want!"

"What if you're a really bad artist?" I asked. "Like Danny?"

"Shut up!" Danny shouted.

"You know you stink at Pictionary!" I yelled back.

"Doesn't matter," Dad said calmly. "We're not

looking for beauty, we're looking for an accurate representation on a four-point scale."

None of us had any idea what that meant, but we all started drawing anyway. This was easy for me. I had downloaded a ton of pictures of toy poodles and saved them in a secret folder on our family computer. (I called it "Zac Efron" just to be sure my brothers wouldn't click on it.)

Mostly what I like to draw is dresses, so I didn't know much about drawing dogs, but I tried to draw Vikki. She's this toy poodle who's won all these awards and has her own website and everything. I love how beautiful she looks. Her teeny tiny paws go pitter-patter when she trots and she is always groomed to perfection. Her soft white fur is practically sculpted, like a sweet little marshmallow around her face, and the pom-poms on her ankles are exactly round. So is the puff on the end of her tail. She is *gorgeous*.

We all handed our drawings in to Dad. When Danny took mine to pass it along he said, "That's not a dog! That's some kind of dumb hedge sculpture!"

"Oh, yeah, what's yours supposed to be?" I shot back. "A mop or a grapefruit?"

"That's enough," Mom said. She and Dad studied the drawings. Mom had brought her laptop in so they could look up all the dogs on the Internet.

"All right," Dad said finally. "Each of you could get a total of four points in this round, one for getting each of these correct: ears, tail, body proportion, and nose shape. Son," he put one hand on Oliver's shoulder, "I'm afraid you get a zero." He held up Oliver's "giant schnauzer" picture.

The drawing had long, floppy ears, a long tail, short legs, and a squashy nose. It didn't look *anything* like a schnauzer, which I know because I looked up miniature schnauzers when I was researching little dogs. In fact, Oliver's picture didn't look like any dog I'd ever seen before. I started laughing.

"All right, fine," Oliver admitted. "I don't know what they look like. I just saw the name on a list of hypoallergenic dog breeds. But come on, you guys! Miru will never come over again if we get something she's allergic to!"

"Boo!" Danny yelled. "You're going to college next year! You shouldn't even get to vote!"

Oliver crossed his arms and sulked while Dad read the rest of the results.

"Miguel, you get two points," he said. "You lost one point because your ears are sticking straight up; Rottweiler ears are small but they flop over. We also docked you a point for making the nose too pointy."

Carlos got three points. He lost one because the

tail on his Border collie was too short and straight, which was dumb because we've all seen *Babe* enough times to know that Border collie tails are long and feathery.

Danny and I both got four points each. Of course, he knew exactly what golden retrievers look like because he'd been hanging out with Merlin 24/7 for two weeks. He was going to be my toughest competition.

So now the chart looked like this:

Name	Breed	Round 1	Round 2	Round 3	Winner
ROSIE	toy poodle	4			
DANNY	golden retriever	4			
CARLOS	Border collie	3			
MIGUEL	Rottweiler	2			
OLIVER	giant schnauzer	0			

"I don't want to play anymore," Oliver said. "I don't care what kind of dog we get. Miru's probably going to break up with me anyway."

We ignored him. Oliver gets moody and ridiculous sometimes. Mom says it's "a teenage thing," but whatever, it's not going to happen to me.

"Round two!" Dad said. "Lightning round! One point each! Name a famous dog of your breed — it can be real or fictional. Miguel, go!"

"Not fair!" Miguel protested. "There aren't any famous Rottweilers!"

I knew I'd seen a couple in movies, but I wasn't about to help him.

"There are some," Dad said, checking the Internet. "Sorry, Miguel. Zero points. Carlos, your turn."

"Fly and Rex from *Babe*," Carlos said promptly. Again, that was hardly fair, since we watch that movie all the time. It's one of the few we all like, because it's not "too babyish" for Oliver and Miguel but it's not too scary for me or too boring for Danny.

"Danny?" Dad said.

"Merlin!" Danny yelled.

"That doesn't count!" I shouted. "Merlin's not famous!"

"He's famous at our school!" Danny pointed out. That was true. Merlin showed up on the playground on the first day of school, and a couple of days later he ran through the cafeteria during lunch and totally started a food fight (I hadn't quite figured out how that happened, but my guess was that Danny was involved). It was a mess and we all had to clean it up, which was gross. Anyway, I figured all that was a sign that Merlin was totally out of control. Did we want a dog like that? I thought not.

"Can you think of a slightly more famous golden retriever?" Dad asked Danny.

"All right, what about that one that plays basketball in those movies?" Danny said. "And there's one on that TV show Mom watches, too."

"He should have to know their names!" I said.

"The judges rule that that's good enough," Mom said. "Point for Danny."

"Miss Rosie, how about you?" Dad asked.

"Vikki," I said, glaring at Danny.

"She's making that up," Danny said.

"I am not!" I said. "She's won lots of dog shows! She nearly won Westminster a few years ago! Mom, look it up."

"She's right," Mom said, tapping on the keyboard.

"Isn't she the cutest thing?" I asked. Mom smiled at me. I had a feeling I was winning her over.

"Famous in the world of toy poodles is not the same thing as *famous*," Danny said.

"At least she has her own website," I retorted. "You can't say that about Merlin!"

"ROUND THREE!" Dad interjected before we started yelling again. "You have two minutes to write down all the reasons you can think of why we should get the kind of dog you want. Feel free to use bullet points and incomplete sentences. As many reasons as you can think of. Go!"

I grabbed the pencil and started writing furiously. On the couch, Carlos and Danny were doing the same. Miguel wrote something down and then stared into the silver pen he was holding as if he was checking out the reflection of his hair.

"Time!" Dad said finally. He took our essays from us.

"Miguel," Mom said, sounding exasperated. "'To meet girls' is not a good reason to get a Rottweiler."

"Sure it is," Miguel said, doing that sideways grin-and-nod that he'd been practicing in the mirror all summer. He doesn't know we've noticed him doing it, but Danny and I make fun of it all the time. He thinks it makes him look like a movie star. We think it makes him look like he can't hold his head up straight.

"I want a tough, manly dog," Miguel said. "Chicks dig that kind of thing."

"Please never say 'chicks dig that' again," Oliver said.

"They do!" Miguel said. "Caitlin and Emma and Sarah will think I'm so cool if they see me walking a big tough dog like a Rottweiler."

"Miru wouldn't be impressed," Oliver said in this superior way, like his girlfriend is cooler than every other girl on the planet. (OK, she kind of is. She has a nose piercing and she draws comic books and wears tall boots and goes to rock concerts all the time. I have no idea why she's dating him.)

"Hmm," Dad said. "All right, he can have one point for that, as debatable as his theory is." Mom raised one eyebrow, but she wrote it on the chart.

Name	Breed	Round 1	Round 2	Round 3	Winner
ROSIE	toy poodle	4	1		
DANNY	golden retriever	4	1		
CARLOS	Border collie	3	1		
MIGUEL	Rottweiler	2	0	1	3
OLIVER	giant schnauzer	0	0	0	0

"Carlos," Dad said. "You list four reasons here, but they all sound like much the same reason to me."

"What?" Carlos said, looking offended.

"Let's see: You say Border collies are smart, it'll be easy to teach them tricks, they learn fast, and we can enter them in competitions."

"Ha!" I said. "You could have just written 'They're smart, they're smart, they're smart, they're smart'!"

"Well, they are!" Carlos cried.

"I'll give you two points for that," Dad said. "Smart and competitions."

Now Carlos looked grumpy, too.

Name	Breed	Round 1	Round 2	Round 3	Winner
ROSIE	toy poodle	4	1		
DANNY	golden retriever	4	1		
CARLOS	Border collie	3	1	2	6
MIGUEL	Rottweiler	2	0	1	3
OLIVER	giant schnauzer	0	0	0	0

"Danny and Rosie," Dad said. He paused dramatically. It's like how he gets all theatrical when he's doing closing arguments to the jury.

"Danny, you write: 'Could be a friend to Merlin.' One point." He paused again. "Rosie, *you* write: 'Poodles don't shed, so she won't make the house messier.' One point."

I wriggled in my seat. This was stressful!

"Danny: 'Goldens are friendly and easygoing.' One

point. Rosie: 'Poodles are hypoallergenic, so our allergic friends can visit.' And you even spelled it right, very impressive. One point."

"*Thank* you, Rosie," Oliver said huffily. Danny and Carlos glared at him, and he added quickly, "But I still don't want a poodle."

"Danny: 'A golden retriever will run around the park and chase tennis balls with me.' Rosie: 'A toy poodle will cuddle on the couch with me and I can dress her up.' Hmmm. I'm not sure either of those should get a point, but we'll give one to each of you and call it even."

I held my breath. Danny and I were tied with eight points. Did he have anything else written down?

"And finally," Dad said, looking each of us in the eye. I think that's a jury trick, too. "Finally, Rosie writes: 'We should get a little girl toy poodle so that there is someone else like me in the house.'"

"What?" Danny yelled. "That doesn't count!"

"It does, too!" I hollered. "You've got Carlos and Miguel and Oliver! I don't have anybody!"

"That's so lame!" Danny cried. "She's saying she should win because she's the only girl!"

"Yeah, Rosie always gets what she wants!" Carlos complained.

"THAT IS SO NOT TRUE!" I bellowed. "Do

you know how much sports TV we watch around here? Or how many boys are always everywhere when I want to have a slumber party? Or how I always have to sit in the middle in the way back of the minivan?"

"Boys, Rosie," my dad said. "Enough! Listen!"

I folded my arms and glared at my brothers. They glared back.

"This contest had many parts," Dad said, "and Rosie has kept up fair and square. This is the tie-breaker, but remember it's not the only point she's scored. And — we're giving it to her. The judges find in favor of Rosie."

"WOO-HOO!" I yelped, leaping out of my chair. I couldn't believe it! I really won!

We were getting a poodle!

"Nooooo!" Danny howled.

"My love life is totally doomed," Miguel said, burying his head in his hands.

"Well, *I'm* not walking it," Carlos grumbled.

"Poodle poodle poodle," I sang, dancing around the room. "Poodle poodle poodle!"

While the boys were complaining, I looked over and my mom winked at me. She knew what it was like. She had older brothers, too (only two, not four, but still!). And I figured she agreed with me about the shedding. It was nice to have a judge who could tell when I was right.

"OK, enough moaning and groaning, boys," Dad said, wiping off the whiteboard. "You all could have won if you'd done your research and thought about it as much as Miss Rosie here." I beamed and fluffed my hair.

"I'll go online tonight," Mom said, "and as soon as we find the right match, we'll get our new dog."

Our new dog!

I didn't care that my brothers were all mad at me. I didn't even care if they never liked my dog. She was going to be *my* dog. And she was going to be perfect. I'd done my research. I'd looked at all the photos of pretty, fluffy poodles online. I already knew what color pink I wanted to paint her nails.

What could go wrong?

CHAPTER 3

We were lucky. (Well, I was lucky. My brothers didn't think it was so great.) My mom found a notice in the local newspaper from a woman whose pet poodle had had puppies three months before. She called, and there was still one puppy left. Better yet, she was a girl puppy, which was what I wanted. We were able to go meet her the very next afternoon.

Oliver decided not to come. He was acting all above us, like he didn't really want a dog anyway. He went for a bike ride with Miru instead.

Carlos stayed home, too. He said he had to study for an exam. This was probably a lie, since there aren't a lot of big tests in the third week of school, but whatever. Since it was just me and Danny and Miguel, I didn't have to sit in the way back of the minivan.

The woman who answered the door said her name was Belinda. She had really short red hair and she was dressed like she'd just been jogging. She seemed really pleased to see us and she told my mom and dad about fifty times that poodles are great pets for a family with kids.

We followed her into the living room, where a little plastic fence was set up in the corner. Inside the fence were a couple of stuffed toys, a water bowl, and a fluffy dog cushion. On top of the cushion was a bundle of white fur.

At first it took me a second to figure out what I was looking at. I had a very clear image in my head of the pretty toy poodle nose and leg puffs and perfect tail. She would be a pure snowy white. But this pile of fur had streaks of honey and tan colors in it, too. And it was all fluffiness.

Then it moved, and I realized that there were two dogs inside the fluff: the mother and the puppy. The mother looked up at us and I realized she didn't have a proper poodle haircut at all. All her fur was the same length, fluffing out around her head and body.

And the puppy was exactly the same in miniature. She let out this tiny yip when she saw us. I could see her little pink tongue as she yawned. She tumbled off the pillow and came stumbling over to our feet. Belinda moved the fence and we all sat down on the carpet.

The puppy blinked big black eyes at us. She kind of swayed in place like she wasn't sure what to do first. Then she shook her head, crouched, and charged at Danny. Only she was too little or too sleepy to run straight, so she wobbled off course and ended up tripping over his sneaker.

"YIP!" she protested, flopping over sideways. She spotted Danny's shoelace and pounced on it like it was responsible for tripping her. She got the shoelace between her tiny teeth and dragged it backward, *grrr*-ing and *snrrrf*-ing and batting at it with her tiny paws.

"Hey," Danny said, trying to get it away from her. She promptly jumped on his hand. The funniest thing was that she was so tiny — she was only about the size of Danny's hand, but she went ahead and bravely attacked it anyway. But she didn't try to bite it; she had her mouth open and kept going "Arrrr arrrr" while she wrestled with his fingers.

I caught Danny hiding a smile.

"She's really *small*," Miguel said disapprovingly. "Will she get bigger?"

"She'll probably be about the size of Muffin here when she's fully grown," Belinda said, pointing to the mother. Muffin was lying on the red cushion with her eyes fixed on the puppy. She looked small enough for me to carry easily — a little smaller than my friend Pippa's cat, Mr. Pudge. So at least one thing was perfect. But I didn't understand why they looked so shaggy. Would it be rude to ask? What if some poodles just grew that way? I couldn't remember reading about different kinds of poodle fur.

Finally I said, "But — why doesn't she look like a poodle?"

"Ah," Belinda said, "you're thinking about the poodles you've seen on TV." I nodded. "That's a particular kind of cut, which is normal for poodles in competition. For Muffin, who's our pet, we just let her coat grow naturally and trim it every few months. And of course, this one's just a puppy. If you want to give her a competition cut when she's older, you can do that. Let me give you her pedigree papers while I'm thinking of it," she said to Mom and Dad. They went into the kitchen and left us with the dogs.

The puppy still hadn't come over to say hi to me. I thought she'd sit in my lap as soon as she saw me. I thought maybe she would lick my fingers delicately a few times and then curl up and fall asleep. Instead she started running in giddy staggering circles around Danny. She kept tripping over her paws and doing little somersaults on the rug. Then she'd bounce up, blinking and looking around like she was trying to catch whoever was doing that to her.

"Come here, Princess," I said, holding out my arms to her.

"Oh, *no*," Danny said. "*Princess?* Are you *serious*?"

I ignored him. "Come on, puppy. Come on, little Princess."

She took a few steps toward me, looking up at me with those enormous eyes. Then she pounced on one of my hands. Her claws were sharper than I expected. "Ow!" I yelped, pulling my hand back. Delighted, she chased after it and pounced again. I held my hands up over my head where she couldn't reach them. So then she tried to climb up my knees. She made it onto my lap, braced her front paws on my favorite pink T-shirt, and leaned up toward my face. Her fluffy tail was swinging back and forth ecstatically. Her little pink tongue snuck out and licked my chin.

"Awww," I said, putting my arms around her and hugging her.

"YIP!" she squealed, scrambling out of my arms and onto my shoulder. Before I knew what she was doing, she buried her nose in my hair, snuffling through my black curls. Suddenly she dug her tiny paws into my shoulder and hurled herself at my pink hair ribbon.

"Eeeeeek!" I yelped as the puppy went tumbling

down my back, yanking on my hair as she fell. She had my ribbon clutched between her two front paws and now she rolled away from me, picked it up in her teeth, and galloped back to Danny.

Danny was actually laughing now. Even Miguel looked somewhat amused.

"Princess!" I said. "Give that back!"

The puppy was thoroughly delighted with herself. She pranced around Danny, bouncing out of reach when he tried to catch her. Her fluffy honey-and-white fur made her look like a little polar bear or a baby seal flopping around.

"Does it have to be Princess?" Danny pleaded. "You got to pick the dog; shouldn't we get to pick her name?"

"No way!" I said. I know my brothers.

"Fuzz," suggested Miguel.

"Twinkletoes," suggested Danny.

"Marshmallow Fluff."

"Foo-Foo the Snoo."

"Señorita Fancypants!"

"Lady Snooty McSnooterfluff of the Waterford McSnooterfluffs!"

"Paperweight!"

"Kickball!"

"Danny!" I yelled.

"No, she doesn't look like a Danny," my brother said, pretending to look at the dog thoughtfully.

"Stop it!" I said. "Her name is Princess!"

"Her eyes look like little black buttons," Miguel said.

"Buttons!" Danny cried. The puppy leaped to her paws and scrambled onto Danny's lap. "See, she likes it," he said. She tried to climb his arm to get up to his face. He picked her up with both hands around her little chest and let her lick his nose. Her tail was going bananas again.

Oh, no. Maybe she *did* like the name Buttons. At least it was better than Lady McSnooterfluff or Kickball. But what about my perfect little Princess?

Mom and Belinda came back into the room. Mom saw Danny holding the puppy and gave me a thumbs-up behind his back. But that wasn't the point at all — Princess was supposed to like *me* best!

And her name was supposed to be *Princess*!

CHAPTER 4

Belinda gave us a dog towel that smelled of Muffin to wrap around the puppy, so she'd have something familiar in her new home. The puppy wriggled a lot as Belinda wrapped her up, but finally she lay still and Belinda put her gently in my arms. A tiny ball of fluff blinked up at me. She was so wrapped up, all you could see was her little fluffy face.

Her eyes and nose did kind of look like buttons — little shiny black buttons buried in a pile of white feathers. She looked like she was smiling at me. She scooted a little forward, motoring her paws inside the towel, and licked my arm where she could reach it. Maybe it wasn't so important to call her Princess.

I thought about it on the way out to the car. I sat in the far back with the puppy while Danny and Miguel took the middle seat. They were trying not to act too interested, but they kept twisting around to look at her.

"You might want to put her on the floor," Mom said to me. "This is her first car ride."

"No!" I said. "I want her on my lap!"

Mom shrugged. "OK, fingers crossed. At least it isn't far."

The puppy rolled around inside the towel as I put my seat belt on. She was making these cute yippy noises and trying to flail the towel off of her, but she just got herself more tangled. I slid her and the towel onto my lap. She managed to wriggle her front paws out and batted at my wrist as the car pulled out of the driveway.

"Shhh," I said, smoothing down the fluff on top of her head. She gazed up at me with her tongue hanging out. Her tiny chest went up and down as she panted.

"Sir Licks-a-lot," Danny suggested, hanging over the back of his seat.

"She's a *girl*," I reminded him.

"Sarah Jessica Paw-rker," Miguel offered.

"Superfluff," said Danny.

"Paw-ris Hilton," said Miguel.

"That's just dumb," I said to him. Danny opened his mouth. "OK, OK!" I yelled, cutting him off. "We can call her Buttons."

"Yeah! Buttons!" Danny said. He and Miguel high-fived. Then they seemed to remember what they were fighting about.

"It's still lame to have a small dog," Danny said.

"Yeah," Miguel said. "I hope the girls at my school don't see it."

"Buttons is not an it, she's a her," I said. "And please, as if any of the girls you like would date you anyway."

"Kids, settle down," my dad said, peering at us in the rearview mirror.

Miguel was about to make a smart-aleck remark back at me, when suddenly he stopped and gave Buttons a horrified look. "What's — uh, what's she doing?"

Buttons had her front paws braced against my thigh. She was making a sound in her throat like *hrrrrrk . . . hrrrrrrrk. . . .*

"Buttons, no!" I shrieked. I grabbed her to move her onto the floor, but before I could, Buttons threw up all over me, the car seat, and my favorite pink T-shirt.

"MOOOOOOOOOOOOOOOOOOOOOOOOO-OOOOOOOOOOOM," I wailed.

"That's what I was afraid of," Mom said grimly.

We pulled into our driveway, and Mom ran inside to get cleaning supplies.

"*Help* me!" I said to Danny.

He shrugged. "I thought you said she was *your* dog."

"Danny, take the dog into the backyard," my dad said.

Danny made a face, but he lifted the towel and the puppy off of me. Holding them out at arm's length, he carried them around the house and into the backyard.

Mom made me clean up the car seat — she said we needed to learn that taking care of a puppy meant lots of cleaning. I didn't like the sound of that too much. I thought a poodle would be naturally clean and pretty and neat. On the other hand, at least having a tiny dog meant there was only a tiny amount to clean up. I consoled myself that this would have been much, much more gross with a Rottweiler.

"Come on, kid," Dad said to me when I was done. "I'll spray you off in the backyard."

I ran around the house while he pulled out the hose. Carlos had come outside, too, and was standing with Danny and Miguel. They were all looking down at something and laughing, which is usually a bad sign with my brothers.

"What's so funny?" I said, coming through the back gate. Then Buttons' head popped up from behind a small pink azalea bush. Her face and paws were *covered* in dirt. It looked like she had been trying to dig her way to New Zealand.

"RUFF!" she announced gleefully and barreled over to me.

"Oh, no you don't," I said, backing up. "You already ruined this shirt — leave my jeans alone!"

But it was too late. Buttons jumped up and planted her tiny paws on my legs. She scrabbled and leaped like she was trying to climb me, squeaking excitedly. Her sweet little ears flapped and her nose went *poke poke poke* against my knee. My jeans were instantly patterned with little brown paw prints.

Then Dad hit me with a huge blast of water from behind. I shrieked and Buttons went wild with excitement. She galloped around in a frenzy, leaping at the water drops and toppling over and skidding on the wet grass with her tiny paws.

"DAD!" I hollered. "You're going to get her ALL WET!"

But it was too late.

CHAPTER 5

By the time Dad turned off the hose, I was dripping wet, while Buttons was dripping wet *and* all muddy. She looked absolutely thrilled. When Dad dropped the hose, Buttons bounced over and tried to attack the end. She went "Rrrrr! Rrrr!" and pounced on it and tried to sink her little teeth into the rubber. Then she jumped back, circled it, and tried to attack it from the other side.

"Stop laughing at her!" I snapped at the boys.

"We're not," Danny said innocently. "We're laughing at you."

Luckily Mom came out through our sliding glass doors before I could shove *him* into an azalea bush. She brought a big orange beach towel for me and a little blue-and-white-striped one for Buttons. We had to chase Buttons around for a while but finally we caught her, wrapped her up, and carried her inside to the downstairs guest bathroom. She looked seriously confused when we put her in the sink. She kept crawling to the edge and peeking over like she thought perhaps she could fly down to the ground. I stayed right next to her to make sure she didn't try it.

Mom brought me the puppy shampoo we'd bought that morning when we got supplies for the new dog. I couldn't wait to put the new sparkly pink collar on Buttons. But I had to get her clean first.

Mom and I poured water on her, making sure not to get any in her ears — Mom said she remembered that from the dogs she had growing up. Rivers of muddy water ran off of Buttons and down the sink. When she was soaking wet she looked even tinier because her fur was plastered to her little body. She didn't like it very much either. She kept wriggling and yipping and trying to take a nosedive out of the sink. I was glad Mom was there to help me keep her still.

"You are a munchkin," Mom said to Buttons in this cute baby-talk voice. "Yes, you are. You're a munchkin." The puppy's wet tail scooted back and forth and splattered me in the face. She beamed at us with her mouth wide open.

I couldn't decide what I thought of Buttons. She wasn't the Princess I had pictured. And this was already a lot more cleaning than I wanted to add to my life. But she was still pretty cute, and I liked it when she licked my fingers or wagged her tail.

Mom wrapped Buttons in a towel and waited while I changed into the dry clothes she'd brought me. Then we put my wet clothes straight into the washing machine and took Buttons out to the living room.

Oliver was sitting on the couch watching TV. He turned it off when we came in.

"Where's Miru?" my mom asked, surprised. "I thought you were spending the whole afternoon with her."

"Yeah," Oliver said, rubbing his hand through his hair and looking mopey. "She had to go home. She didn't say why."

"Oh," Mom said. "That's too bad."

"Well, that's OK," I said. "Now you can meet Buttons. Buttons, this is Oliver." I have to admit, I was kind of hoping Oliver would like Buttons. I figured she'd have the best chance with him, since he's not *quite* as annoying as all my other brothers. Sometimes he even lets me play on his computer while he's doing homework, as long as I'm quiet.

I set the towel-wrapped puppy down on the couch next to him.

"Wow, that is small," Oliver said, but before he'd even finished the sentence, Buttons was burrowing her way out of the towel. She pushed it away from her with all her paws and started rolling madly on the couch. Her fur was fluffing and spiking out in all directions. Her paws flailed in the air. She spun in a circle, one way and then the other, and then tried to bury her nose in the dark blue cushions.

Suddenly she spotted Oliver and threw herself at his hand. He flipped it over so it was palm up and rubbed her belly as she sprawled across it. She stretched out her paws in both directions and then flopped over sideways so she was pinning his hand down.

"Hmm," Oliver said noncommittally, but he didn't take his hand away. I sat on the couch on the other side of Buttons and scratched her tummy and her ears. Her tail swished happily across the blue fabric. And guess what? Not a single hair was left behind. OK, there were a couple of wet patches where she'd rolled vigorously, but at least that was just water.

"What's Lady McSnooterfluff doing now?" Danny asked, coming into the room.

"Buttons!" I said. "I agreed we could call her Buttons!"

"All right, all right," Danny said. He hovered beside the arm of the couch, watching Buttons like he wanted to pet her, too, but didn't want to admit it. Finally he made a weird face and said, "Mom, can I go hang out with Parker and Merlin?"

"Sure, dear," Mom said. "Be home for dinner, or call me if you won't be."

Almost as soon as Danny had clattered out the back door, Carlos appeared in his spot. He also kept staring at Buttons.

"How did your studying go?" I asked sweetly.

"Oh . . . fine," he said. "Can she do anything yet?"

"Let's give her a day to settle in," Mom said. "We can start training her tomorrow."

Carlos shifted his feet. His hands twitched like he wanted to pet her, but he eventually shoved them in his pockets and wandered back upstairs.

Buttons was fast asleep by the time Miguel came in. All the excitement of meeting us and throwing up in the car and digging and getting wet and then getting bathed had apparently worn her out. One little ear was flopped back cutely so you could see the pink underside. Her front paws were crossed like she'd just fallen over that way. And she was making this tiny *snnzzzz . . . snnzzzz . . .* sleeping sound with her nose.

This was more like what I had imagined from my dog. Peace and snuggling.

Miguel shook his head. "My reputation will be ruined if anyone sees me with that dog," he said.

"What reputation?" Oliver said. "The girls at school don't even know you're alive."

Miguel scowled, which made me think Oliver was probably right. "Well, they'd notice me if I went running by with a big manly dog!" Miguel sputtered.

"A big manly dog wouldn't fit in the bathroom sink," Mom pointed out calmly.

"Hrrrmph," Miguel said, and stalked out of the room.

"Belinda said that Buttons has been pretty good about housebreaking so far," Mom said to me, "but we have to keep it up by letting her go outside every couple of hours. So keep that in mind when she wakes up."

"OK," I said. Mom left us there and went off to get some work done. She owns a clothing boutique in town and she's always looking online for interesting new designers to include. I think one day I might be a fashion designer. My favorite TV show is *Project Runway*. My signature style will be that all my clothes will be pink or sparkly . . . or pink *and* sparkly!

Oliver turned the TV back on with his free hand and flipped it to a documentary about baby polar bears. He still didn't move his hand out from under Buttons. I kept petting her. It's OK to be quiet with just Oliver.

"Girls are weird, Rosie," Oliver offered during a commercial break, about half an hour later.

"Nuh-uh," I said. "*Boys* are weird. There's this boy a grade below me, Isaac, who is *constantly* bothering me and stealing my ribbons and making me chase him and it's *so* annoying. Why would he do that? Right? Only explanation: weird."

"He probably likes you," Oliver said, staring at the TV.

"Ew, *gross*," I said, horrified. "He's *nine*. And he always has *chocolate* all over his face. EW. Seriously. Ew." I paused. Oliver didn't seem to be listening to me anymore. "You never did that to Miru," I tried. That got his attention.

"Well, I'm not in fourth grade." He let out this long-suffering sigh. "And whatever I *am* doing isn't working. She doesn't like me anymore."

"Did she say that?" I asked.

"No," he said. "I can just tell." He let his head fall back on the cushions and stared gloomily up at the ceiling.

"Well, do something about it," I said. "Don't let her go. She's probably the coolest girl who'll ever agree to date you."

Oliver sighed again. "I know."

"Rrrrft," said Buttons. I looked down at her. She had her head raised a little bit and was watching the TV screen. Two polar bear cubs were rolling around in the snow. "Rrruff!" Buttons said again. It was like she wanted to bark but wasn't sure she really wanted the bear cubs to turn around and notice her. So she settled for a kind of curious half bark. "Rrrruff!"

"She's watching the TV!" I said, impressed. "Isn't she clever!"

"I watch a lot of TV, and I'm not very clever," Oliver said, but he kind of smiled at Buttons.

"Maybe she thinks they look like her," I said.

She kept her bright black eyes on the polar bear cubs for a while. Finally she scrambled up to her paws and started exploring the couch. Oliver flexed his hand, shook it, and then patted her back as she stuck her nose between the cushions. Her tail went *flap flap flap*. Now that she was mostly dry, she was back to being fluffy and cute and (mostly) white. Her ears were just a little bit darker than the rest of her, like fuzzy tan caterpillars on either side of the white puff-ball of her head. Her chest was mostly white, while the rest of her was like honey and milk mixed together, like white with a hint of gold in it. If she could stay that color instead of getting all muddy again, I'd be perfectly happy.

"Stay there, Buttons," I said, getting up and going over to the bag of stuff we'd bought at the pet store. There was a little thump behind me and I turned around to see that she'd launched herself off the couch. She sat on the carpet blinking and looking dazed for a second, then remembered what she was doing and galloped over to me.

She kind of threw herself over my arm and nearly did a head plant into the shopping bag. I held her back with one hand while I fished her collar out.

"Look how cute!" I said to her. "Pink and sparkly!" She sniffed it dubiously, then grabbed it in her teeth and shook it as hard as she could.

"Shush," I said, prying open her jaws and getting it back. "It'll be gorgeous on you, just wait." I'd really wanted to get some of the little pink jackets and shoes and things I saw in the pet store, but Mom said we should wait and see how big Buttons was first. She said it in that way she does when she's hoping I'll get distracted and forget, but it didn't work when I wanted to be Princess Jasmine from *Aladdin* for Halloween, and it wasn't going to work now. I was going to get

Buttons into a cute outfit no matter what Mom did or how much the boys whined about it.

For now I would settle for the pink collar, if I could get it on her. Buttons pounced on it and wrestled with it and rolled on it and tried to eat it and basically did everything except sit still to let me put it on her. But finally I got it latched around her neck. She kept turning in circles trying to look at it.

"You look adorable," I said proudly. "I'll show you." I picked her up and carried her out to the full-length mirror at the end of the hallway. I put her down and pointed at the mirror. She jumped on my finger and tried to chew on it. I pulled my hand free, took her between my hands, and pointed her at the mirror.

"RRUFT!" Buttons barked, suddenly spotting her reflection. "RRUFT! RRUFT!" Her little paws motored back and forth but I was still holding her, so they just flailed in space above the carpet. "RRUFT!" Buttons insisted again. She wanted to go play with the dog she could see in the mirror.

Carlos poked his head over the banister. "What's she doing?"

"Saying hello to herself," I said. I let go and Buttons leaped down the hall. She bounced up and planted her front paws on the mirror. When the "other dog" did the same thing, she leaped back, spun in a circle, and then crouched with her head down and her butt up in the air.

"That's a play bow," Carlos said in that superior, *I-know-everything* way that he has. "It means she wants to play."

"Well, duh," I said.

Buttons stayed that way for a minute. Her tail swayed back and forth. She made this tiny little growl deep in her throat. But the "other dog" didn't move either. Finally Buttons pounced at the mirror and jumped back again. Then she trotted up and sniffed the glass, jerking away whenever she thought her reflection was getting too close. In the end she tried to poke her nose behind the mirror to find the dog but, of course, there wasn't anything back there.

"It's OK, Buttons," I said. "You can play with me instead."

Losing interest in the boring mirror dog, Buttons trotted back down the hall, sniffing the carpet intently. Soon she found herself at the sliding glass doors to the backyard. Her ears perked up. A couple of sparrows were hopping around on the lawn. Buttons sat down and stared at them.

"You want to go chase them?" I asked. She looked

up at me with her tongue hanging out. Her front paws were planted between her back paws. She was really the cutest pile of fluff when she was clean.

I leaned over her and opened the door. Buttons scrambled out onto the lawn and galloped after the sparrows. I was about to follow her outside when the phone rang.

"Rosie!" Dad called. "It's for you!"

Our yard has a fence all the way around it, so I knew Buttons would be OK outside for a minute. She was sniffing the lawn intently where the sparrows had been. I ran to get the portable phone.

"Hello?" I said.

"Hey, Rosie." It was my friend Pippa. She's kind of the opposite of me in a lot of ways. She's really pale and really quiet. She has perfectly straight hair down to her waist that is such a pale blond it's almost white. I wish I could be quiet and sweet like her sometimes but, hello, she doesn't have any siblings, so she has an advantage. It's much easier to be quiet and good when you don't have big hooligans dropping spaghetti in your hair or cutting butt flaps in all your Barbie dresses (true story).

"Hi, Pippa!" I said. "Guess what?" I didn't wait for her to guess. It takes eons for Pippa to guess whenever I say that because she thinks for a really long time, although she'd probably come up with the right answer in the end. "We got a dog!" I squealed.

"You did?" Pippa said. "That's so amazing! What kind?"

"A poodle puppy," I said. "She's so cute. You should come over tomorrow and meet her. We can dress her up together."

"OK!" Pippa said. "I'll ask my mom."

I wandered over to the glass doors while we talked. When I peeked outside, I couldn't see Buttons right away.

"Hang on a sec," I said. I slid the door open. "Buttons!" I called.

"Aww, that's the cutest name!" Pippa said. "Buttons. I love it. I wonder if Mr. Pudge will like her."

I heard a small *rrrrrrrrft* from behind that same azalea bush. Then I spotted dirt flying up in the air. Uh-oh.

"BUTTONS!" I yelled.

Her little face popped out. Except now it didn't look like the cute, clean face I'd let into the yard. Dirt was smudged into her whiskers from one ear to the other. She grinned goofily at me.

It wasn't even two hours since her last bath, and already she was a muddy mess again!

CHAPTER 6

I told Pippa I'd call her back, and then I went into the yard and chased Buttons with a towel. She loved that. She galloped back and forth, ducking away every time I dropped the towel on her. Then she grabbed one end of the towel in her little teeth and went "Rrrrr! Rrrrr!," trying to shake it back and forth. Finally I got her wrapped up, but she managed to poke her face out and lick my ear as I carried her inside, which left a trail of dirt down the side of my neck. And when she tried to wriggle free she left more muddy paw prints on my second set of clothes for the day.

"Whoa," Oliver said, passing me on his way to the kitchen. He could see Buttons' muddy face and paws sticking out of the towel. "That was fast."

"Will you help me give her another bath?" I pleaded. "I don't want to bother Mom again."

"Yeah, OK," he said. We put Buttons in the bathroom sink again. She tried to bite the water coming out of the faucet and then got very confused when it went up her nose. She sneezed *SNFFFT! SNFFFT!*, and then shook her head vigorously. Her ears went flippity-flap and spattered water everywhere.

I couldn't believe we'd only had this dog for three hours. It felt like I'd spent almost that whole time cleaning up after her.

"And you got your pretty collar all dirty," I cried. "Buttons! Very bad!"

She licked my fingers and gave me this big-eyed *sorry* face.

"She's just being a puppy," Oliver said. "I think that's normal."

I took a deep breath. "Still better than a Rottweiler," I said. It was important to keep reminding myself. "Imagine trying to give a dog like *that* a bath every two hours."

Oliver actually cracked a smile. Normally he only does that when Miru is around.

Finally we wrapped her in yet another towel — it was a good thing that we had so many old ones, in a house with this many dirty boys — and I carried her up to my bedroom. Oliver brought the pet store bag up and left it with me.

As I mentioned before, my room is the cleanest one in the house. There is a big sign on the door which I made myself using pink poster board and glitter. It says NO BOYS ALLOWED. ESPECIALLY DIRTY ONES. In smaller letters at the bottom, which I had to add later, it says ESPECIALLY DANNY! DANNY, THIS MEANS YOU! That's because Danny pesters me more than any of the others. He's always trying to come in and mess up my toys. As you can probably guess, he was responsible for the whole Barbie-butt-flap catastrophe.

I'm always like, "If you want to play with me, just *say* so!" but then he's like, "No way! Blah! Girls are stupid!" Which is, like, so mature. Whatever. I bet he *wishes* he could have Barbies and My Little Ponies.

I think part of why he's such a huge pain is because he has to share a room with Carlos, while I get my own room because I'm the only girl. Next year Carlos will move into Oliver's room, so maybe then Danny will get a life and stop bothering me.

A couple years ago, Mom helped me decorate my whole room to be exactly the way I wanted. The carpet is a pale pink color, like the inside of seashells. The wallpaper is white with tiny pink rosebuds on it, and the curtains are lace with pink ribbons tying them back. I have two small heart-shaped shag rugs on the floor that are bright, bright, *bright* pink, which matches my hot-pink rolling desk chair.

On one wall there's a bookshelf where all my dolls and stuffed animals are perfectly placed, and on the other wall is the bookshelf with all my books, arranged alphabetically by author. The nice thing about my books is that a lot of them were bought new for me, because the boys never wanted to read *Eloise* or *Madeline* or *Fancy Nancy* or *A Little Princess* or *Pippi Longstocking* or *Allie Finkle*, and my mom was really excited to get them all for me. So I didn't have to inherit all the books my brothers destroyed growing up. I swear, I think they used them for tennis rackets instead of reading them.

I have a couple of poodle pictures that I printed out from the Internet pinned to the bulletin board above my desk, next to my Hello Kitty calendar and some of my fashion drawings. I don't have a computer of my own yet, but I'm hoping Mom and Dad will let me have Oliver's when he goes away to college next year, because then he'll probably need a new one.

My bed has a white headboard and footboard, which I have covered in sparkly pink stickers. I make my bed every morning because it looks neater that way. I like smoothing out the wrinkles in the pretty pink polka-dot bedspread and then putting my fluffy pink throw pillows on top with my three favorite stuffed animals.

I set Buttons down on the carpet and closed the door behind me. She tumbled out of the towel and started rolling and wriggling across the carpet, trying to get dry. I opened the pet store bag and pulled out the dog bed we bought for her. I knew I wanted this one as soon as I saw it. Of course, it was pink, but even better than that, it had little sparkly rhinestones around the outside of it and tiny little dark pink dog bones printed on the inside. A ring of soft fluffy white fur went around the top.

"Look, Buttons," I said, putting it down next to my bed. "This is for you!"

Buttons ignored me. She'd just spotted one of my pink shag rugs. With a tiny "RRFT!" she pounced on it. Her little claws went *dig dig dig dig dig!* She grabbed on to a tuft of pink fur with her teeth and tried to shake it. To her surprise, the tuft came right out of the rug. Buttons tipped over backward and blinked, looking startled. Then she dropped the tuft, yipped in delight, and dove on the rug again.

"Buttons! No!" I shouted. She was going to destroy my rug! I scooped her up and pried another tuft of pink fur out of her jaws. Then I dumped her on the bed while I picked up the two shag rugs, folded them, and hid them at the back of my closet.

"Yip!" Buttons announced cheerfully and pounced on one of my pillows. "Grrr! Yip!"

"Quit that," I said, picking her up again. She

agreeably went all floppy and started chewing on my thumb and staring into space like she was daydreaming. I carefully put her into her new little bed and sat down on the floor next to her. She was so tiny it made the dog bed look huge. You could fit ten little Buttons-size dogs in there.

Buttons stood up and walked around the edge of the bed, sniffing in all the corners. She poked her nose over the top and blinked at me. She looked like she was thinking, *What the heck is this for?*

"Isn't that sweet?" I said. "Don't you love it? It matches your collar, Buttons! Well, it did before you got your collar all dirty, you bad puppy."

Snnrrrrft! Buttons sneezed again. Maybe some of the white fur had tickled her nose. She sat down, sniffed at her tail for a moment, and then bounced back onto her paws. With a determined look, she headed straight for the edge of the dog bed and tumbled off onto the carpet. Pleased with herself, she jumped up and marched away across the floor, nose down like she was exploring. I watched her sniff every inch of the room. Finally she stopped by the door and flopped down on her tummy with her paws stretched out in front of and behind her. She closed her eyes and sighed in a contented way. She looked like she was smiling. And falling asleep.

"Oh, Buttons!" I said, exasperated. "You're supposed to sleep in your *bed.*"

But I didn't want to wake her up again, so instead I finished my homework and read the new *Allie Finkle* book until dinnertime.

Buttons woke up when my mom called me for dinner. She sat up quickly like she couldn't remember where she was. The fur on one side of her face was all smushed up and funny-looking from lying on it for so long. She blinked and shook her fur out and gazed up at me. Then her mouth opened and her tongue lolled out and she looked like she was beaming. Almost as if she'd recognized me and it made her happy.

"Time to go outside again," I said. "And this time I'm coming with you!"

I carried Buttons down the stairs because I thought she was probably still too small to manage them by herself. Dad saw me coming and ruffled the fur on Buttons' head as we went by. He grinned. "She's a cute one, all right," he said. "Has she been good up there?"

"She's been sleeping, mostly," I said.

"Aw, that makes sense," he said. "I think puppies sleep a lot — especially when they've had an exciting day like this one."

"Plus two baths!" I said. "Even *I* don't take two baths a day!"

Dad chuckled. "I must say, this is the first time I've seen you in a dirty shirt — at least, since you were a toddler, I think."

I realized I'd forgotten to change again after Buttons' last bath. What was happening to me? I always changed *immediately* if I got anything on my clothes. I even took an extra shirt to school in my backpack, just in case of a lunch disaster (like, say, a food fight started by a crazy dog).

"Well," I said, "I guess she might get me dirty again." But I was determined not to let that happen. I carried Buttons right out the sliding door into the yard and set her down on the lawn.

"Here," I said, pointing to the grass. "Keep your paws clean. No digging." Buttons tilted her head at me. She looked like she was waiting for me to do something. "Go on," I said.

The glass door slid open and closed behind me. I turned and saw that it was Oliver. "Keeping an eye on her?" he asked.

"And that azalea bush," I said. Just as I said that, Buttons made a break for it. I jumped in between her and the bush and she skidded to a stop, blinking up at me with this baffled expression. "Oh, no you don't," I said. "Be good, Buttons!"

She tilted her head the other way, as if she was thinking, *What do you mean? I AM good!* This seemed to give her a lot to think about for a minute or two. Finally she sauntered off across the grass, sniffing and pawing at the ground and doing her business.

"There," I said, satisfied. "Problem solved."

"Mm-hmm," said my brother.

We watched her nose closer and closer to the flower beds on the other side of the lawn. I was ready to run across and grab her if there was any sign of digging. Slowly she sniffed one clump of grass . . . then the next . . . now she was standing right next to the edge of the mulch my mom put down around her violets and begonias. Mulch is like a mix of dirt and wood chips, as far as I can tell. Would Buttons want to dig in it?

Buttons peeked over her shoulder at us.

"Don't even think about it," I said, putting my hands on my hips.

Buttons looked back at the mulch. I took a step toward her. Buttons snuck a glance between her legs to see if I was coming. Then she flung herself down on the mulch and began rolling. *Rolling!*

Glorious, wholehearted, enthusiastic flailing around in the dirt!

"BUTTONS, NO!" I shouted. I ran over just as she flipped herself upright again and shot past me. Clumps of dirt and bits of wood were tangled all through her fuzzy white coat. More dirt was stuck to the bottom of her paws. She galloped around me and charged right at Oliver.

"Hey!" he said, dropping to his knees. Buttons leaped onto his lap and jumped up, trying to lick his face. He picked her up in both hands and held her at arm's length. She wriggled and scrabbled at the air, trying to get closer to his nose. Her pink tongue went in and out as she frantically licked the air.

Oliver started laughing.

"It's not funny!" I said. I stomped up and tried to pick the mulch clumps out of her soft curly fur while he held her. Seriously, she'd only had about ten seconds of rolling time. *How had she made such a mess?* And more importantly, why did she want to? Why couldn't my dog be more like me?

What was wrong with her?

CHAPTER 7

It was kind of a relief to go to school the next day. I loved Buttons, but we had to give her two more baths before bedtime. Then she didn't want to sleep in her pretty pink dog bed at all. She whimpered for a while, trying to get up on the bed with me. But Mom said I absolutely could not let her sleep on the bed until she was definitely house-trained. So I put her on the floor and finally she crawled under the bed and fell asleep on the carpet.

Mom snuck into my room in the middle of the night to let her out again, just to be safe, but I thought maybe Buttons was already ready to sleep through the whole night. Why she didn't want to sleep in her bed, though, was a mystery to me. It was *so* pretty! And pink! How could Buttons not love it?

The next morning we all ran around getting ready for school, as usual. It's always total chaos in my house in the morning. There are only three bathrooms upstairs, and I'm not even kidding, Miguel takes, like, an *hour* in there, making sure this one little strand of hair at the front of his head swoops in just *exactly* the right way or something. Oliver always has to bang on the door and yell at him.

I usually sneak through Mom and Dad's room and use their bathroom, which is the cleanest anyway because they don't leave wet towels on the floor and tiny shaving hairs in the sink and dirty sneakers scattered around, like *some* people I could mention.

Buttons loved the chaos. She ran around under everyone's feet, attacking shoelaces and yipping excitedly. When I let her out, she didn't even go roll in anything, because she just wanted to come back inside as fast as she could. She didn't want to miss any of the crazy action going on.

Mom only goes into her store a couple of days a week — she has a manager who runs it day-to-day, so she can do the business stuff at home. So she was going to take care of Buttons during the day. I told her I hoped Buttons wouldn't need too many baths while I was gone.

"It's OK," Mom said, rumpling the puppy's fur. Buttons snuggled up close to Mom's foot. "I think we'll have fun today, won't we, sweetie?"

"Mom, what kinds of dogs did you have growing up?" I asked.

"Small fluffy ones," she said, with a twinkle in her eye. "Maltese and Yorkie mixes, mostly."

"Aha," I said. I was starting to think Mom had been on my side all along. And since she would be taking care of her so much, I thought it was only fair that we had won.

"'Bye, Mom!" Danny yelled, hurtling out the back door and grabbing his bike. He rides over to Parker's house every morning so they can go to school together. Which is fine by me; I don't need to show up at school with my big noisy brother. Instead Pippa's mom always picks me up and drives me.

"There she is," Mom said, glancing out the window. She handed me a paper bag with my lunch in it. Danny buys his lunch at school, but I make my own sandwiches the night before because I think the school lunches are kind of gross and sloppy-looking. Also, I like to have the crusts cut off and the edges perfectly aligned and the exact right amount of peanut butter or mustard, depending on which kind I decide to have, pb & j or ham. No one else makes my sandwiches quite the right way, not even Mom, who at least tries.

"'Bye, Buttons," I said, crouching down to pet her. "Be good! Oh, Mom, can Pippa and Michelle come over after school?"

"Yes, if their parents say it's OK," Mom said. "Hurry now, don't be late."

I grabbed my pink Powerpuff Girls backpack and ran down to Mrs. Browning's car. As usual, Pippa was in the front seat and our other friend, Michelle, was in the back. Pippa waved at me as I got in.

"Pippa says you got a dog," Michelle said right away, without waiting for a hello or anything. "Is that true, Rosie? Did you get a dog? What kind? What's it like? Why did you do that?"

Michelle always asks a lot of questions. I think it's because she's practicing. Her parents are both psychologists (or psychiatrists, I forget the difference), and she wants to be one, too, when she grows up.

One of the things I like about Michelle is her fashion sense. She has this great puff of curly black hair which she always ties back with different colorful scarves. Her dad's family still lives in Kenya, and I think they must send her scarves for every birthday and holiday, because she has, like, a kajillion of them. This morning her scarf was orange and yellow in kind of a bird pattern. She was wearing a matching orange shirt and a blue jean skirt.

As usual, I was wearing pink. This was my fourth-favorite pink shirt, since my first- and second-favorites were still in the laundry, covered in tiny paw prints, and I wore my third-favorite on Friday. I keep track of these things.

"I *did* get a dog," I said. "You guys should come over after school and meet her. Morning, Mrs. Browning."

"Morning, Rosie," said Pippa's mom.

"Is that OK, Mom?" Pippa asked.

Her mom said yes, like I knew she would. Pippa comes over to my housc most days after school because her mom often works late and Pippa doesn't like being home alone. Her dad died a long time ago, so it's just her and her mom and Mr. Pudge now. And no offense, but that cat is not exactly Excitement-O-Rama.

"I'll call my dad from school and ask him. So tell us more about the dog," Michelle said. "How do you feel about it? Do you like her? Do you feel that she is jiving with your family dynamics?"

"What does that even mean?" Pippa asked.

"It means how do your brothers feel about it," Michelle explained. Sometimes I think Michelle likes Danny. She talks to him way too much when she comes over. I've told her all the terrible stories about him, but that doesn't seem to bother her.

"They wanted a big dog," I said, "but I won, so we

got Buttons, who is teeny tiny. She's like this big." I held up my hands to show them. Pippa went "awww" and Michelle grinned. "You guys will like her," I said. I didn't tell them about her dirt problem. Maybe it was just a first-day thing. Maybe she'd be over it by the time I got home.

We're all in Ms. Applebaum's class, which is lucky. Last year Pippa was in a different class from us and I missed her — Michelle is great, but she's impossible to pass notes with because hers are all full of questions and big words she picked up from her parents.

Ms. Applebaum's big thing is "making a difference" and she's always organizing projects for us to "help the community." Our first homework assignment on the first day was to think of something we could all do to make the town or the world a better place. Then we had to write an essay about why we should do it.

I said we should all go clean up a park or a beach or something. I always see trash on the ground, even in our really nice park, and I figured it would make the town better if we all got together and picked it all up. Then after I finished the essay I had another idea, so I wrote a second essay about how we could take old clothing donations and fix them up so people who needed clothes would actually want them. I said we could patch holes or sew new buttons on old coats or add fun patches and sequins to pants and dresses and skirts. Mom even said her store could help us.

Ms. Applebaum really liked that idea, so we'll probably do it later this year. She put it on her Big List, which is a huge scroll of paper on the bulletin board at the front of the room, where we can all see it all day long. I was amazed at how many different ideas the other kids had. Some of them were about the environment, like recycling and changing lightbulbs and biking or walking instead of driving. Someone said we should plant trees or flowers around the town to make it greener (although it's pretty green already). Someone else said we should take turns visiting and playing with the animals at the local pet shelter, Wags to Whiskers.

Michelle's idea was that we should do a bake sale and use the money to buy a goat for a family in Africa. She even brought in pictures from when she visited her family in Kenya last year. It was really cool and we all liked the big smile on her grandmother's face and the two cute little goats in the background. So that's the one we all voted that we wanted to do first.

Ms. Applebaum got really excited about "global responsibility" and how little things we do can make a big difference to someone all the way around the world, because now that family can send their kids to school or something. I wasn't sure if the kids were going to be too thrilled about that (like, "Gee, thanks, America!"), but at least they'd be getting a cute goat to play with.

The bake sale was going to be that Friday. We were planning to set up a table during lunch and also after school, so we could sell stuff to parents, too. Dad said he'd help me make peppermint meringue cookies on Thursday night, which I was excited about because they'd be different from everyone else's brownies and chocolate chip cookies.

Anyway, for math we practiced adding and subtracting and giving change, like if someone wanted two cookies that were twenty-five cents each and they gave us five dollars, how much would we give back, stuff like that. It was a lot more interesting than just sitting and writing down numbers. I got to be the customer a couple of times, so I pretended to think really hard and change my mind seven times the way my dad would. Everybody laughed, which was cool.

Whenever we had a break, I thought about Buttons, and the more I thought about Buttons, the more I looked forward to going home. I was sure that the first day she'd just been nervous and excited. Now she'd be calmer. She'd lie on my lap and be good and quiet. Pippa and Michelle and I would dress her up and she would keep her delicate paws clean and be a sweet angel. Everything would finally be perfect.

I bet you can guess just how wrong I was about that. . . .

CHAPTER 8

It was raining when Mom picked us up after school. I was disappointed that she didn't have Buttons in the car with her, but when she reminded me of the puppy's *last* car trip, I decided she'd made the right choice.

Michelle and Pippa and I ran to the car holding our backpacks over our heads and jumped in.

"Danny wants to go to Parker's," I said to Mom. "He says he wants to play with a *real* dog, not a stupid ball of fluff. Those were his exact words."

Mom rolled her eyes. She knew I was trying to get Danny in trouble. "All right," she said. She waved at Danny through the windshield and he waved back, then climbed into Troy's car with Troy and Parker and Eric. Danny's friends are all much quieter and nicer than he is. I don't understand why I couldn't have one of *them* for a brother instead.

I actually think Eric Lee is kind of cute (not that I'd ever admit that to Danny!), although most of the girls in my class are absolute idiots about Parker Green instead. Apparently he's, like, "the dreamiest, cutest, smartest, nicest, handsomest boy who ever lived," according to them. But I've seen him yelling at video games and spilling strawberry ice cream on his shirt at our house, so I know he's just a regular guy — which is to say, noisy and messy.

Eric, on the other hand, is usually pretty quiet, and I think if you can find a guy like that, you should hang on to him, because there aren't many. I'm not really interested in boys right now, 'cause I totally don't have time for them, but I have this whole plan where I'm going to date Eric once we're both in high school. I figure by then he won't think of me as Danny's annoying little sister anymore. And hopefully he'll still be polite and quiet like he is now. I keep an eye on him to make sure he isn't turning into a regular dopey boy.

When we got home, Oliver was already there. He always gets home first because the high school lets out half an hour before our school, and this year he usually came home right away to work on college applications. He was totally stressing about them, which is silly because he's perfectly smart.

We walked into the living room and caught Oliver rolling on the rug with Buttons. She was trying to climb over him, but he kept rolling so she'd topple off or get carried over to the other side. She was wagging her tail like crazy and going *arrrraaarrraarrrr*, and Oliver was laughing. Which, like I said, was amazing because he's usually all serious all the time.

He didn't even look embarrassed when he saw us. He sat up and Buttons came careening over to crash into my feet. She wrapped her little front paws around my ankle and tried to chew on my shoelace.

"Oh, she's so cute!" Pippa said. She sat down on the carpet and let Buttons sniff her hand.

"Wow," Michelle said, flipping her scarf over to the other shoulder. "I can't believe how small she is."

"I know," I said. I scooped Buttons up in my hands. She felt like a little ball of feathers. "Come on, let's go upstairs. I want to see if any of my doll clothes will fit her."

Oliver winced. "Oh, Rosie," he said.

"She'll like it!" I said. "She'll look so cute!" I didn't wait for him to answer. He didn't know anything about being cute and pretty. I marched upstairs with Buttons and Pippa and Michelle and shut the door to my room so none of my brothers could bother us.

"Oooo, I like her bed," Pippa said, patting the fringe of white fur and admiring the rhinestones.

Michelle sat down on the floor, and Buttons immediately pounced on the end of her scarf.

"Hey!" Michelle yelped, grabbing her hair. Buttons rolled over so the scarf was on top of her and her paws were in the air. All we could see was a little lump under the orange fabric, wriggling and going *rrrr! rrrr!*

I ran over to my dresser and pulled out five different pink ribbons. I also took a couple of dresses off my dolls that I thought would fit Buttons perfectly. One of them was pink with lacy sleeves. I knew it would look *so* cute on her.

Pippa and I sat down next to Michelle and I lifted the scarf off Buttons. The puppy sat up and blinked at us like, *Whoa! Where did you guys come from?*

"Look, Buttons," I said, picking up the most sparkly ribbon. "Isn't this adorable?"

Buttons didn't think it looked adorable. She thought it looked delicious. She seized the other end in her teeth. Michelle and Pippa both had to help me get it away from her without ruining the ribbon. Then they held her still while I took the fluff of fur on top of her head and bunched it into a little puffy ponytail. I wrapped the ribbon around the fluff, and Pippa tied it in a pretty bow.

Buttons kept twisting her head about, trying to figure out what we were doing. I tucked the ends of the ribbon behind her ears so she couldn't tug on them and pull it loose. Then I took the lacy pink dress. It closed with Velcro in the back, so I just put the front sleeves over Buttons' front legs, wrapped the dress around her body, and stuck it together along her back. It fit just as perfectly as I thought it would. She looked like a tiny pink princess.

"It's perfect!" I squealed.

Except for one thing. Buttons wouldn't sit still in it. Michelle held her while I got my camera, but still Buttons flailed all her paws and twisted and tried to chew the sleeves. All my photos of her looked like sparkly pink-and-white blurs.

"I don't think she likes it," Pippa said, sounding worried.

Just then there was a knock and my bedroom door opened. Buttons thrashed extra-hard and popped out of Michelle's hands. As my mom poked her head inside, Buttons shot through her legs and tore off downstairs.

Mom's mouth dropped open. "What did you do?" she asked.

"Nothing!" I said. "We just made her prettier!"

"MOOOOOM!" Miguel hollered from downstairs. "Something ENORMOUSLY EMBARRASSING is running around our living room!" I heard boys laughing and guessed that some of

Miguel's friends were here. I could also hear Buttons yipping as she ran.

"Santa Maria!" Carlos yelled. "What did Rosie do to the dog?"

Then there was a huge clatter like books getting knocked off the coffee table. Mom and my friends and I all ran down to the living room.

Buttons was tearing around in huge circles like wolves were chasing her or something. She didn't even seem to notice that she'd crashed into the coffee table and knocked everything off. The ribbon was hanging down in her eyes and her claws had caught on the lace of the dress so it was half torn off and trailing behind her. Part of it was wrapped around one paw so she couldn't run straight. Her yips were getting louder and faster and more frantic.

Miguel and two guys from his class were sitting on the couch with their feet up out of her way. They were all laughing so hard they could barely talk. Carlos was standing in the door to the kitchen with his arms folded. He didn't look like he thought it was funny.

"Buttons!" I shouted. "Stop! Sit! Be good! Stay still and be pretty!"

"All right, that's enough," Mom said. She stepped forward and caught Buttons as she zoomed around the couch. Mom lifted her up and Buttons tried to burrow into Mom's shirt. With a quick tug, Mom pulled off the ribbon and then the dress, disentangling it from the puppy's claws.

Buttons' tail started to wag and she stretched up and started licking my mom's chin like it was a melting ice-cream sundae.

"It's all right," my mom cooed. "Yes, it's all right, Buttons, you're a good dog."

"She's not a good dog!" I said. "She tore my dress! She pulled off the ribbon I picked for her!"

"That was so lame," Carlos said. "You actually made me feel sorry for that fuzzball."

"Rosie, let's go talk in my room for a minute," Mom said. "Pippa, Michelle, I put out some cheese and grapes and crackers in the kitchen."

"Yum," Michelle said, and my friends both went off to find the snacks while I followed Mom up to her room. Mom sat down on the floor and let Buttons go. Buttons started trying to bury her face in the carpet. She planted her head on the floor and pushed herself along with her back paws, then stopped and went *dig dig dig dig dig* with her front paws. Her fur stood up in funny spikes around her face.

"Rosie, *chiquita*," Mom said. "You can't put any more dresses on Buttons."

"But why?" I said. I started to cry. I didn't want to — I hate crying — but it wasn't fair! Buttons was supposed to be the dog *I* wanted, and the dog I wanted was supposed to like pretty dresses and ribbons . . . not rolling in dirt!

"She's a puppy, not a toy," Mom said, pushing my hair back from my face. "You mustn't force her to do things she doesn't like. How would you like it if someone dressed you up against your will?"

"I'd like it if the dresses were pretty and pink like that one!" I said, crying harder.

"Buttons doesn't know or care about being pretty," Mom said. "She's a dog — she just wants to have fun and play with you in fun puppy ways."

"She won't anymore," I said. "Now she's going to hate me."

"Are you kidding?" Mom said. "Buttons loves you. Here, give her this, and she'll forgive you right away." Mom fished a dog treat out of her pocket and put it in my hand. Buttons sat up as soon as she smelled it. Her little black nose went *sniff sniff* and wiggled in the air.

I held out my hand to her. She bounced over and snarfed up the treat. Her tiny pink tongue licked my hand clean. Then she let me scratch behind her ears. She gave me that look like she was smiling again.

"Maybe she didn't hate it so much," I said hopefully.

"No, Rosie," my mom said. That's the voice where I know I can't win. "No more dresses on the dog."

I blinked back the rest of my tears. Why couldn't things be the way I imagined? I'd won the contest to pick the dog, but I was starting to feel like the biggest loser of all.

CHAPTER 9

Pippa and Michelle didn't say anything about the dress when I came back downstairs. Michelle didn't even ask any qucstions. I think they weren't sure if I was in trouble or not. We finished our snacks and then Mom said we could practice teaching Buttons to come when she was called.

Miguel and his friends were in his room "doing homework," which I think really means "talking about girls," but at least they weren't in the living room anymore. So each of the three of us and Mom took a bunch of dog treats and sat on the floor in a big square. I held Buttons on my lap while we got settled. She kept licking my hand and wagging her tail, so I guess she wasn't too mad at me anymore.

Of course, I wasn't exactly sure that I wasn't still mad at *her*.

Mom called her first. "Buttons, come here!" she said, holding out her hands. "Buttons! Come!"

Buttons sat down on my foot and panted, looking up at me.

"Go on," I said, pointing at Mom.

Mom pulled a treat out of her pocket. "Buttons!" she called, but before she'd even finished saying it, Buttons galloped across the carpet to her and leaped at the treat. "Yes! Good girl! Good Buttons!" Mom said happily, patting her while Buttons ate the treat. "Now you, Pippa."

"Buttons!" Pippa called. Buttons' ears went up and she tilted her head at Pippa. "Buttons!" Pippa called again. Buttons took a tentative step toward her. Then Pippa held up the treat, and Buttons sprang into action. She ran over so fast she tripped over her paws and did a kind of somersault into Pippa's lap. "Aww, good girl, Buttons," Pippa said, patting her.

Michelle had to hold up the treat to get Buttons to come to her, too. But when I called her, Buttons ran right over to me without waiting to see if I had a treat. She bounced around my feet with all of her fur going *sproing! sproing!* "Good girl! Good Buttons!" I said, letting her have the treat.

We did that for ten minutes, until Buttons would come to each of us no matter who called her or in what order. We started giving her treats only every other time and she still came, and she still looked really delighted when we told her how good she was.

"Aren't you a clever, clever girl?" Mom said to Buttons, rubbing her tummy as Buttons rolled on the floor.

"Huh," Carlos snorted from the doorway. I didn't know how long he'd been watching us. "Sure," he said, "she'll go to you now that she knows you have treats. That doesn't mean she knows her name."

"You call her then," Mom said. "Try it."

"But sound excited," I said. "Act happy to see her."

Carlos rolled his eyes. "Buttons," he said in this bored voice. "Hey, Buttons." The puppy sat up and looked at him. Her ears twitched. Carlos looked surprised. "Buttons, come," he said with a little more enthusiasm. He reached out a hand toward her.

Buttons scrambled to her paws and charged across the carpet to him. She pounced on his hand, wrapped her front paws around it, and started trying to lick it into submission.

"Wow," Carlos said. "That actually worked!"

"Of course it did," Mom said proudly.

"Buttons, sit," Carlos said. He held his hand above Buttons' nose. She tried to jump up and touch it, but he lifted it out of reach and then down again, holding it right over her nose and moving it back. Slowly her butt went down. It touched the floor. Buttons was sitting!

"How did you do that?" Michelle gasped.

"That was so cool!" Pippa said.

"Good sit, Buttons," Carlos said. Mom tossed him a treat and he gave it to Buttons. She chewed on it with this cocky expression, like, *Bring it, mister, I'm a genius.*

"Huh," said Carlos. "I saw that on a TV show, but I didn't think it would work."

"I told you poodles are smart," I said (OK, a little smugly).

Mom checked her watch. "We should let her out again," she said.

"But it's raining!" I said. "She'll get all wet!"

"She has to get used to it," Mom said, shaking her head. "We don't want her to think she can pee inside whenever it's raining."

"All right," I said with a huge sigh. "Come on, Buttons."

Buttons trotted to the sliding doors with me and pawed at the glass. Rain was splattering down through the trees. I could see that the grass was soaking wet.

"OK, but come right back," I said to her. She gazed up at me with her tongue hanging out. I opened the door and she scrambled outside. I closed the door again and peered at her through the glass.

At first Buttons seemed surprised by the water coming from the sky. She shook her head and then shook it again and then spun in a circle like she thought maybe her tail was to blame. I couldn't hear her, but I knew she was *grrrr*ing and yipping. Her fur was already getting plastered to her little body. I pulled the door open a little ways.

"Hurry up, Buttons!" I yelled.

She stopped spinning in a circle and looked over at me. I shut the door again so I wouldn't get wet. Buttons blinked and started padding across the lawn. Her paws went *sploosh sploosh* in the wet grass. She stopped and did her business and then kept going. She sped up a little as she headed for the flower bushes. Suddenly I saw what she was aiming for.

"Buttons, NO!" I shouted, throwing the door open again.

Buttons ignored me. She dove headfirst into the enormous mud puddle at the edge of the lawn. The mud went *SPLOOSH!* all over her. Thrilled, Buttons flipped onto her back and started rolling with glee.

"Buttons!" I yelled. "Buttons! Bad dog! Buttons! Stop it!"

It seemed like Buttons couldn't even hear me through the rain. Or else she had too much mud in her ears. Her paws flopped around as she wriggled deeper into the puddle.

"MAN!" I shouted, slamming the door shut. I ran and got my raincoat and galoshes. Mom followed me to the door and saw what Buttons was doing. She hid her smile, but I saw it.

"Look how bad she's being!" I said. I sat down on the floor to pull my boots on.

"She's just having fun," Mom said. "She doesn't know it's bad. Like when you were little and you had no idea that throwing peas at your brothers drove me crazy."

"Well . . ." I said, "but that's different. Peas are gross. And mud is gross! Why does she like it so much?"

"It probably feels new and goopy and exciting," Mom said. "Like when you met Jell-O for the first time."

I didn't remember that, but there were pictures of me in our family albums with my face and hands and high chair covered in shiny grape-flavored speckles. All right, fine. So even I played with my food when I was little. But I got over it pretty fast!

I pulled the hood of my raincoat up and ran out

into the yard. Buttons didn't see me coming. She was having far too much fun covering herself in mud. When I scooped her up, she didn't look anything like herself. She was muddy and dripping from tip to tail. And she had the most enormous grin on her face.

"What are you doing?" I asked. "Why are you crazy?"

Buttons draped her paws over my arm and snuggled into my chest. I could feel her heart beating through my fingertips. She was so little. Maybe Mom was right and she really didn't know she was being bad. But how could I get her to stop?

Pippa and Michelle thought muddy Buttons was the funniest thing they'd ever seen. They stood around the sink and helped me while I gave her *yet another* bath. I left my raincoat on so my clothes underneath wouldn't get wet. Buttons didn't even try to jump out. She was too interested in exploring my friends' hands to see if they were hiding any more treats.

Finally she was clean again. We wrapped her in a towel and took her into the living room, where she promptly fell asleep on the couch. Soon after that, Michelle's dad picked her up, and then Pippa's mom called to ask if Pippa could stay for dinner, since she was stuck at the office. So Pippa and I did our homework in the living room, next to sleeping Buttons.

"You're so lucky," Pippa said out of the blue while I was working on a Spanish work sheet. I like those because they're easy for me — my grandparents on Mom's side only speak Spanish, so I've spoken it since I was little.

"Lucky? Why?" I said. "I'm totally not. Have you met my brothers? It's like torture living in this house."

"It seems like fun," Pippa said wistfully. "It's always really quiet in my house." It sure wasn't quiet here. I'd been wondering whether Pippa could really concentrate on her homework with all the noise going on. I mean, I'm used to it but, for instance, right at that moment, Miguel was blasting his music upstairs, Oliver was in the downstairs office talking to Miru on the telephone, Carlos was watching TV in the den, and Mom was clattering around in the kitchen. I was pretty sure deaf people three blocks away could hear my house.

"And now you have a dog, too," Pippa added. She patted Buttons, who went *snnzzzrr snnzzrrt* in her sleep and rolled closer to Pippa's hand. "I wish we could have a dog."

"What kind would you want?" I asked.

“I don’t know,” Pippa said. “One that gets along with Mr. Pudge. Maybe a poodle like yours.”

“Hmph,” I grumbled. “You should get a *real* poodle instead. Want to see pictures of what they’re supposed to look like — when they’re not all muddy and wet?”

“OK.” Pippa followed me into the den and I opened my file of photos on the family computer. Carlos turned up the volume on the TV and ignored us. He was watching something on the History Channel. Seriously! As if he could get any more boring.

I clicked on a photo of a toy poodle at a dog show. She looked so perfect and neat and precise. Nothing like the snoozing ball of fluff in the other room.

“Isn’t she precious?” I said to Pippa.

“Yeah, that’s what I thought Buttons would look like,” Pippa said. “I mean, I thought all poodles looked like that.”

“Me too!” I said.

Carlos glanced at us, flipped off the TV, and left the room. Fine with me. I always feel like I’m winning when I can get my brothers to go away. Especially since they just ignore me when they’re in the same room as me anyway.

"Let's pick out a dog for you," I said, clicking on the Internet. "There are so many cute little ones."

I showed her Malteses and Yorkies and shih tzus and Pomeranians and papillons and all these cute mixes of little dogs that were really sweet, too. Pippa giggled and went "Awwww!" at every photo. She liked the papillons best because of their funny big butterfly ears and tiny faces, so we decided she should get one of those.

After about half an hour I left her at the computer and went to check on Buttons.

And guess what I found?

Carlos was playing with her!

CHAPTER 10

AHA!" I cried. "You like the dog! You do! You loooooove her!"

"I do not!" he said, jumping to his feet. His face was turning red. "I just wanted to see what other tricks she could learn."

Buttons was sitting politely on the couch next to him. She looked over her shoulder at me with this serious *Excuse me, I'm very busy learning here* face.

"Is it working?" I asked.

Carlos rubbed his head. "Yeah, I guess," he mumbled.

"Like what?" I said. "Show me."

Carlos was acting all "whatever" but I could tell he was actually kind of excited. "Buttons, shake," he said, holding out his hand.

And Buttons *put her paw in his hand*!

"Oh my gosh!" I yelped. "She did it!"

"Good shake," Carlos said, giving Buttons a treat.

She stood up and gobbled it out of his hand. "We're working on 'stay,'" he said to me. "Buttons, sit." He did the same hand motion as before and she sat down again on the couch cushion. "Buttons, stay." He put his hand out flat toward her. Then he took a step back. And another step. Buttons sat still, staring at him. I was practically holding my breath. He took another step back. Buttons was quivering with excitement.

"Good stay! Come here!" Carlos said. Buttons flew off the couch and ran over to him. She jumped and leaped around his feet as he dropped treats in her mouth.

"So she is pretty smart, huh?" I said.

"I guess she's pretty smart," Carlos admitted. "I only have to show her about six or seven times before she gets it."

"Show me how to teach her tricks," I demanded. "I want her to know everything."

"We should take her to a class when she's a little older," Carlos said. "When I thought we were going to get a Border collie, I found these tricks and obedience and agility classes not too far away. Maybe Buttons wouldn't be too bad at them."

"She'd be amazing!" I said. "I bet you she'd be top of her class."

"That'd be kind of cool," Carlos said. He smiled at Buttons. Yeah, he totally did.

I was proud of my little dog. But it made me a little grumpy, too. Buttons was acting like exactly the dog Carlos had asked for. So why couldn't she be more like the dog *I'd* dreamed of?

Just then Mom called us into the kitchen to get our plates for dinner. Buttons came romping along with us, *rrrrrrft*ing excitedly. I was about to tell Mom about her brilliant tricks, but then Buttons accidentally careened into her food dish, knocked all the kibble into her water bowl, spilled all the water on the floor, and somehow managed to get wet kibble crumbs all through her fluffy fur.

So it didn't seem like the best time to tell everyone how smart she was.

Carlos told Danny a little bit about it at dinner, though. Danny went "ha" and said, "Any dog can learn to sit. *Merlin* can catch a tennis ball in his mouth *in midair*."

"Ooooo, all hail the great and wondrous *Merlin*," I said. Pippa giggled.

Carlos gave Buttons a thoughtful look, like he was thinking about how to train her to do that, too. I thought it might be hard, since her head was only about the size of a tennis ball itself.

"Yeah, well, a Rottweiler can tear off your hand with one bite!" Miguel said with relish.

Pippa looked horrified and so did Mom. "I don't think that's true," Mom said.

"OK, I made it up," Miguel said. "But they *look* like they can!"

"You're deranged," I said to him.

Oliver didn't say anything. He was moping again. I guess his phone call with Miru had gone badly.

After Pippa went home, I went back to the computer and looked at the photos of poodles again. Maybe I would feel better once we could give Buttons a proper poodle haircut. Even if she couldn't wear a dress, she could at least have cute little puffs of fur around her ankles.

Danny and Oliver came into the den to watch a baseball game, and Danny spotted the photo I had open.

"Oh, man," he said. "What are you plotting now?"

"This is what a poodle *should* look like," I said. "See how pretty and delicate she is? This will be Buttons as soon as she's old enough for a haircut."

"That dog looks completely ridiculous," Danny said. Oliver made a face and nodded, which made me mad. I was hoping Oliver would support me, since he seemed to actually like Buttons.

"Buttons is going to look like a little princess!" I said. "Even if I can't put ribbons on her!"

"What are those?" Danny demanded. He leaned over my shoulder and pointed at the round, fluffy rosettes on the top of the dog's hips. "Are those BUTT PUFFS?"

"They're not *butt puffs*," I said. "They're *rosettes*."

"*That* is a puff of fur on either side of the dog's butt," Danny said. "Those are BUTT PUFFS. You want our dog to have BUTT PUFFS."

"I think they're pretty!" I said.

Oliver slapped his forehead and sat down on the couch, shaking his head.

"Well, I don't care," Danny said, turning away. "It's not *my* dog anyway."

That's right, I thought. *She's* my *dog. Or she's supposed to be. Even if she won't wear pink.* Then I had an idea. Mom said no dresses . . . but maybe there was another way to make Buttons a little more pink and princessy.

After school on Tuesday I went up to my room. Pippa had her after-school art class on Tuesdays, so she wasn't there with me. I took that class with her last year, but I only wanted to draw pretty dresses with neat pencils and markers, and the teacher made me do all these messy things with clay and paste and glue and watercolors, and I ruined a perfectly nice pink skirt that way, so I told Mom I didn't want to do it anymore.

I opened my bottom dresser drawer and pulled out a big clear box. Inside, all my nail polish is arranged by color: pale pinks in the top row, bright pinks in the middle, and reds at the bottom. I love painting my nails. I'm the only girl I know who can keep my nail polish from chipping for four whole days straight. Except when bratty Isaac steals my ribbon and I have to chase him around the playground — that usually ruins my nail polish, which is another reason why it makes me so mad.

I picked out two bright pinks and two pale pinks and took them downstairs to the living room. I just had to decide whether to do all of Buttons' nails the same color, or different for each paw. It was going to look so cute! I was really excited. Then my dog and I would have matching nails and everyone would be able to tell that she was *mine*.

Oliver was sitting on the couch letting Buttons chase his hand around in circles. She would play-growl and pounce on it, and then he'd sneak it away and hide it under a cushion, and she'd go *dig dig dig* with her little paws trying to get to it. When I came in, he had just flung a blue cotton blanket over her head. The blanket-covered blob was yipping and leaping about like this was the most thrilling thing that had ever happened to her.

Oliver spotted the nail polish in my hand before I even said anything. "Uh-oh," he said.

"Don't you try to stop me," I said, wagging my finger at him. "Buttons will love it!"

"Buttons will *hate* it," Oliver said.

"Hate what?" Carlos said, coming in from the yard. His eyes went straight to the nail polish in my hands. "No! Rosie, no!"

"SHE'S MY DOG!" I yelled. Buttons popped her head out from under the blanket. Her fur was all fluffed up around her face like she'd gone through a dryer. She yipped when she saw me and came to the edge of the couch, leaning toward me and wagging her tail.

"See?" I said. "She's excited." I sat down on the floor, but then I remembered that Mom always makes me spread out an old towel under my hands when I paint my nails. Which is silly, because I am the only person in this house who can actually manage *not* to spill something, but I follow the rules so she'll keep buying me new polish. So I got up and went out to the linen closet to get a towel.

When I came back, my four bottles of nail polish had mysteriously vanished.

"Oliver!" I said. "Did you take my nail polish?"

"What nail polish?" he said innocently. Buttons rolled over and Oliver rubbed her tummy. I couldn't tell from his face whether he was really the thief or not.

"Carlos, give it back," I said, putting my hands on my hips.

Carlos lifted his hands in the air. "I don't know what you mean," he said.

I stamped my foot. "Where is it? Give it back!"

"I'm pretty sure this is a nail-polish-free zone," Oliver said. Carlos nodded.

"You're not going to stop me," I said, pointing at them. I turned and ran upstairs. I had more nail polish. I was *going* to do this. Most importantly, I was going to do this before Mom got home from the boutique. I wasn't sure if she'd stop me, but I *was* sure that if she saw how cute it looked *before* she could stop me, she'd let me do it again.

I pulled out a few more bottles of pink nail polish and ran downstairs. Now my towel was gone. Buttons sat on the couch blinking at me like, *What's all the running around for?*

"Stop it!" I shouted at Carlos and Oliver, stamping my foot. This time I took the nail polish with me when I went to the linen closet. When I got back to the living room, Miguel and Danny were there, too. It's like some kind of smoke signal goes up when one brother is torturing me; somehow all the others suddenly turn up to join in.

"*Tell* me you're not going to do this," Danny said, frowning at the nail polish.

"A Rottweiler would bite your hand off if you tried it," Miguel offered, making things up again.

"Well, it's a good thing we have Buttons instead of a Rottweiler!" I snapped. I spread the towel on the floor in front of the couch and sat down on it. I set one of the nail polish bottles right next to me. My brothers all hovered around staring.

"Buttons, come here," I said, patting the towel.

"Don't do it, Buttons!" Danny cried dramatically. But Buttons jumped down onto the towel and came over to sniff my hand. I patted her head.

"Good girl," I said. "Now sit."

Buttons tried to chew on my thumb. "No," I said, pulling my hand away. I made the hand gesture I'd seen Carlos do. "Sit." Buttons tilted her head at my hand, and then sat.

"Man. I feel like my powers are being used for evil," said Carlos.

"Buttons, shake," I said, holding out my hand. Buttons lowered her head and licked my palm. Carlos snickered, so I just picked up Buttons' paw. She sat there and let me hold it. Her tongue was hanging out and she smiled up at me. See, I knew she could be a good dog.

"Good girl," I said. I reached for the nail polish with my free hand.

It was gone!

I felt around the towel looking for it, but it had vanished just like the others. I hadn't even noticed my brothers moving. One of them must have darted forward to grab it while I was looking at Buttons.

"You guys are so mean!" I said.

"You're the one that's mean!" Carlos said. "Doing something like this to poor Buttons."

"You don't understand because you're a boy," I said, trying to sound all superior the way he usually does. "Buttons is a girl, like me, so she'll like having pretty pink nails."

"I don't think that's how it works," Oliver said. "I

mean, she's a dog. Why would any dog want their nails painted? It's going to look silly, Rosie."

"No, it *won't*," I said. I didn't have to argue with them. I had another bottle of nail polish in my pocket. When I pulled it out they all groaned, but I ignored them. I shook it and then twisted off the cap carefully, scraping the brush against the side of the top so it wouldn't drip.

Of course, I had to let go of Buttons' paw to do that. Buttons sat still for a moment, but once the nail polish was open, she tilted her head and stood up. She took a small step forward and sniffed at the bottle.

SNNNNZZZT! She sneezed loudly and with enough force to knock herself over on her butt. I grabbed for her paw, but she bounced up and backed away.

"Buttons, come here," I said, holding the brush in one hand and reaching for her paw with the other. Buttons took another step back, looking from me to the brush with a wary expression.

"Seriously, Rosie," Oliver said.

"It's not like you need to make her *more* embarrassing," Miguel said.

"Shut up!" I said furiously. "Buttons, COME HERE!"

Buttons hesitated for another moment, then turned and fled around the back of the couch.

My brothers exploded into cheers.

"WOOO!" Danny shouted. "Buttons does something right!"

"She proves she's smart again!" Carlos cried, applauding.

"Yeah!" Miguel yelled. "Run, Buttons! Run for your life!"

"Shut up!" I screamed. "You guys are SO MEAN!"

I jumped up and stormed out of the room. I threw the nail polish brush in the sink on the way upstairs. I didn't feel like going back to save the rest of my nail polish, which I figured my brothers would hide as soon as I left.

I was mad at my brothers, but I was more mad at Buttons. She ran away from me! Why didn't she want to do anything *I* wanted to do? How dare she agree with my brothers? The whole point was that I was finally supposed to have someone on *my* side! Someone else small and girly and pretty, who didn't need to make a lot of noise and mess to have fun.

Someone who would like me better than anyone else.

Instead I had a terrible feeling that Buttons didn't like me at all.

CHAPTER 11

I sulked in my room for a while, but that got boring, especially after I ran out of homework to do. I tried changing the dresses on my favorite dolls to make myself feel better, but I was sick of all my dolls and their boring dresses.

I wanted to play with Buttons.

But I was pretty sure Buttons didn't want to play with me. I kept remembering the look on her face before she ran away behind the couch.

After about an hour, I was ready to go downstairs, but I didn't want to if my brothers were just going to laugh at me. I opened my bedroom door and listened. Miguel's music was playing from his room. And there were shooting/zapping noises coming from the den, so someone was playing video games. That meant at least two brothers were out of the living room, which meant only half the teasing.

I snuck down the stairs and peeked into the living room.

Carlos and Oliver were in there with Buttons. I watched for a minute. Carlos had an old sock in his hand. He threw it to Buttons. She jumped up and tried to catch it, but it flopped over her eyes. With a *grrrft!* she bounced sideways and shook her head until it fell off. Then she grabbed the sock in her teeth and shook it until it was dead, and then a few more times for good measure.

Then Oliver tried to take the sock away, and they played tug of war with it for a while. Buttons went *rrrrRRRRrrrrRRRRrrrrRRRR* like a toy car revving up as she tugged and tugged on it. But Oliver snuck it away from her when she let go for half a second.

"YIP!" Buttons protested, jumping on his knees. Oliver tossed the sock to Carlos.

"Buttons!" Carlos called. "Buttons, catch!"

Buttons threw herself in the air as the sock came flying toward her. This time it landed neatly in her jaws. She looked as surprised as anyone.

"RRRFT!" she mumbled triumphantly around a mouthful of sock. She shook the sock vigorously again.

Carlos and Oliver laughed and clapped. I wanted to cry. That wasn't my dog in there. I was the one who had to give her a bath every time she went outside, but then she spent all her time playing stupid boy games with my stupid brothers. It was like my brothers were this special club I was never allowed to join, but now Buttons could be part of it and I still couldn't. I mean, not that I wanted to, but still. Stupid, noisy, messy club.

I stomped into the room and threw myself down on the couch. Buttons dropped the sock and sat up to look at me, but I didn't say anything to her or to my brothers. I flipped on the TV and turned on *High School Musical*, which was still in the DVD player because Pippa and I had put it in to watch our favorite scene on Monday. I know my brothers hate it, which is just one of many reasons why I love that movie.

"Buttons is being really good," Carlos said to me. "She's caught the sock lots of times. Want to see?"

I turned up the volume on the TV and crossed my arms.

Oliver and Carlos played with Buttons a while longer, and then Oliver took her outside while Carlos went upstairs to study. When Buttons came back in, she wasn't even all muddy. Apparently that was only something she did when *I* had to clean her.

Buttons trotted in through the door ahead of

Oliver and bounded over to me. She sat at my feet and gazed up at me.

I kept my eyes on the TV, ignoring her.

"Aroo aroo," whimpered Buttons. She put one paw on my foot. When I still wouldn't look at her, she pawed at me insistently. "Arooo."

Oliver was leaning in the doorway now, looking at us.

"Oh, all right," I said, picking Buttons up and plopping her on the couch beside me. Wagging her tail excitedly, Buttons came over and climbed on my lap. She had to push her head under my elbow to get there, but she was determined. Once she was in between my arms, she turned in one direction, and then the other, and then she curled up in my lap with her head resting on my left knee. She let out a contented huff.

"Awww," Oliver said.

"Sure, I can be her pillow," I said. "That's all I'm good for."

"Rosie, Buttons loves you," Oliver said. "She wants to play with you. She just wants to play dog games, not people games."

"She doesn't love me," I said. "She hates me. She ran away from me." I stroked her soft little head.

"She didn't run away from *you*," Oliver said. "She ran away from the nail polish. Remember, dogs have a really strong sense of smell. It probably scared her."

Buttons shifted and rolled toward me so her paws were in the air and her head was flopped back. I rubbed her tummy and she wriggled happily.

"Oh," I said. I didn't think of that. I'm used to the smell of nail polish by now, but I guess it is pretty strong. "Maybe if she gets used to it, then?" I said.

"I don't know, Rosie," Oliver said. "Think about this — what if she tries to lick it off before it dries? That would be really bad for her. Like poison."

"She wouldn't do that!" I said. "Would she?"

"Maybe not," Oliver said. "But it could get on her fur, and dogs lick themselves all the time. I wouldn't risk it."

I felt awful. I hadn't thought for one second that Buttons would do something like that. I definitely didn't mean to put poison on her nails. Poor Buttons!

"I'm sorry, Buttons," I whispered, scratching her tummy with one hand and tickling her chin with the other. Buttons nudged my hand until she got it to where she could lick it, and then she licked my thumb all the way around. She did like to lick. Poor baby.

"OK, Buttons," I said. "No nail polish for you."

Oliver smiled.

"Hey, Oliver," I said as he turned to go, "um . . . maybe don't tell Mom about this?"

"We won't," Oliver promised. And when Oliver promises something, all the other guys go along with him.

Buttons and I snuggled on the couch until dinnertime. She didn't even jump down to say hi to Mom and Dad when they came home. She just wanted to sleep on my lap and get petted. I felt much better by the time I went to bed, but I still wished there was something to make me feel like Buttons was really *my* dog.

On Wednesdays my mom spends the whole day at her boutique, so usually Michelle and Pippa and I walk down there after school, since it's not very far. I love being in the store with all the pretty, fancy clothes. Mom lets us try things on if we're careful. She calls me her "brilliant little helper" when I arrange the shoes and accessories for her.

When we walked into the boutique on Wednesday afternoon, the little bell over the door jingled and I heard a "RUFF!" from the back of the store.

Pippa looked at me. "Was that —?"

Buttons came flying out of the back room and threw herself at my legs, jumping and wriggling and yipping like she hadn't seen me in years.

"Buttons!" I cried. "What are you doing here?"

The store manager, Ashley, leaned over the counter and smiled at my puppy. "Isn't she a sweetheart?" she said. Ashley has spiky short blue hair and this funny British accent that we all think is probably fake. She spent, like, one summer in England, four years ago, but otherwise she's always lived here. She loved it over there, though, and now she drinks a lot of tea and talks like the Queen of England. Like, she calls cookies "biscuits" and sweaters "jumpers" and sneakers "trainers," which is just funny, if you ask me, and probably confusing for some of the customers. But she's also really nice to me, so I like her, especially when she calls me "luv," as in: "Hand me that jumper, would you, luv? Cheers!"

"Your mum brought her in for the day," Ashley said. "She's been a right star with all our ladies. Haven't you, luv?" she cooed at Buttons.

"Aww, are you popular?" Michelle asked Buttons, scratching behind her ears.

"I'd buy whatever you're selling," Pippa agreed.

"A classic psychological marketing strategy," Michelle said. I could tell she was about to explain whatever that meant, so I jumped in and cut her off.

"Mom, we're here!" I called.

"Be right out!" she called back.

"She's measuring Mrs. Perlman for some alterations," Ashley explained. Mrs. Perlman is one of my mom's best customers because the boutique will adjust anything for free if it's bought there. Mom just takes the customer into the back room and does some measuring and cutting and stitching and it's like a miracle how suddenly any dress can look good on someone. Mrs. Perlman is short and very round and really pretty, and she can never find anything that fits her anywhere else. But everything Mom fixes up looks amazing on her.

That's one reason I like fashion. I think the right clothes can make anyone look and feel prettier. I'd love for someone to put on a dress I designed and say: "Wow, I feel beautiful now." Mom gets that reaction all the time when she alters dresses for her customers. And I want to make dresses for people that are all shapes and sizes, like me and Pippa and Michelle and Ashley and Mrs. Perlman are. Of course, they all have to like pink. But who doesn't?

"Let's see if there are any new earrings," Michelle said, heading over to the accessory wall. I picked up Buttons and brought her with us. She felt like a teddy bear in my arms, all soft and floppy and snuggly. She poked her nose under my chin and licked my neck, wagging her tail like that was her funny way of saying hello.

Pippa doesn't have pierced ears yet, but Mom makes sure the store carries clip-on earrings, too. Sometimes I think she does that because she noticed that Pippa was feeling left out, but I'm not sure if that's too much like thinking Mom has magical powers. Anyway, we found some pretty, dangly ones and were taking turns lifting them up to our ears and looking in the mirror when the bell over the door jingled again.

I turned around and saw that it was Miru, Oliver's girlfriend. She actually comes into the boutique a lot. My mom is really good at picking clothes both for teenagers and grown-ups. That's how Oliver and Miru met — he was at the store helping Mom change the artwork on the walls. He was up on a ladder holding a Frida Kahlo print while Mom said: "That way a bit . . . no, the other way . . . OK, down an inch," when Miru walked in and started laughing at him. Blah blah, love at first sight, whatever.

"Hi Miru!" I said.

"Hey Rosie," she said, coming over to us. "Hi Pippa, hi Michelle." See how cool Miru is? She even remembers her boyfriend's little sister's *friends'* names. "Is this your new puppy?" she asked.

"Yeah, this is Buttons," I said, flapping one of her paws at Miru.

"Oh my *goodness*, you're cute," Miru said to Buttons. She rumpled Buttons' fur around her face, and Buttons wagged her tail.

"Oliver's not here," I said.

"I know," Miru said with a huge sigh. "He had to go home and work on 'college applications.'" She put finger quotes around the words.

"He's really worried about them," I said.

"Well, so am I, but I still want to spend time with him!" Miru said. "I mean, it's like he can't wait to get out of here and away from me." She started flipping through the rack of dresses on sale. I followed her with Buttons in my arms.

"That's crazy," I said. "He talks about you, like, *all the time*. It'd be annoying if you weren't, like, so awesome."

Miru grinned at me. Her nose stud today was a little green emerald that sparkled in the overhead spotlights. I wish my hair were straight like hers and Pippa's; mine has these waves in it that I can't get rid of.

"Well, when the boys start lining up to date you, Rosie, just remember to go for one that can actually express his emotions, OK? Like, one who actually cares about stuff and can say he does instead of being all serious and focused on his work and blah blah blah."

I didn't know what she meant. Did she think Oliver was like that?

"Rosie," Michelle called before I could ask Miru any more questions. "Are these earrings really five dollars?" She held up a pair of dangly copper-colored lightning bolts.

"If that's what thc tag says," my mom said, popping out from behind the curtain to the back room. She smiled and said hi to everyone. Mrs. Perlman followed her out and went up to the counter with a huge pile of clothes. I think the store would survive even if Mrs. Perlman were the only customer.

"That's it? Oooh, I want them!" Michelle said, digging in her pocket for money.

Pippa looked down at the earrings in her hand, then put them slowly back on the shelf.

"Five dollars?" Mom said, taking the earrings as Michelle handed them to her. "I think we can make these a present, Michelle dear. It'll be a celebration of our new family member." She patted Buttons' head. "Pippa and Rosie, you can each pick out a pair from that shelf, too."

"Really?" I said.

"Sure," Mom said, her eyes twinkling, "but don't you go for the expensive ones on the next shelf, Miss Rosie!"

"I won't!" I said. I already knew I wanted the ones that looked like little pink pearl raindrops. I put Buttons down on the floor so I could pick them up. Next to me, Pippa picked up the ones she'd been holding again. They each had a pretty dark sparkly blue stone in the middle with lacy silver flower petals around it.

"Wow, Pippa, those are so you," I said. I helped her clip them onto her ears and she looked at herself in the mirror, tucking her pale blond hair back so she could see them.

"Thanks, Mrs. Sanchez," she said with a smile.

"Yeah, thanks, Mrs. Sanchez!" Michelle said.

Suddenly there was an enormous *CRASH* from behind the curtain. We all looked around in surprise, and I realized that Buttons wasn't at my feet anymore.

"Uh-oh," I said.

CHAPTER 12

"YIP! YIP! YIP!" barked something in the back room.

I got to the curtain first, and when I pulled it back, I saw Buttons tearing around the room with a purple knit hat stuck over her head. It was covering her eyes, so she kept crashing into things as she ran. She'd already knocked over Mom's mannequin and a stack of hatboxes. I jumped in to rescue her, but she raced between my feet, got tangled in a long dress hanging from a rack, dragged it behind her past the table, and sent a whole carton of sewing supplies flying. Safety pins, buttons, and needles scattered everywhere.

"Buttons!" I yelled. "Buttons, STOP!"

"Buttons, shh," Mom said calmly. Buttons stopped running when she heard her voice. She pawed frantically at the hat on her head, then lay down and started rolling and rubbing it into the carpet, trying to shove it off.

Mom stepped over the fallen mannequin and whisked Buttons up off the floor before she could step on any pins and hurt her tiny paws. She pulled off the hat, and Buttons pawed at her nose with both paws, looking bewildered.

"Heavens!" Ashley said in her funny accent.

"Wow," Miru said. "That was a fast-acting disaster."

"Poor munchkin," I said as Mom put her in my arms. "You are the silliest dog I've ever met. AND the messiest! Look what you did!" The back room was kind of a catastrophe. Buttons buried her face in my shoulder like she didn't want to look at it. Her heart was going really fast and her little chest went up and down, up and down as she panted.

So of course we had to spend the rest of the afternoon cleaning it up and picking buttons out of the carpet. Pippa and Michelle were really helpful. We took turns keeping Buttons out of the way while the other two put things back together. At the end, Mom said we really earned our earrings and she wanted to buy us ice cream, too. Which was very nice, considering it was my dog that had caused all the mess in the first place, but I didn't remind her of that!

So we left Ashley to close the boutique and walked up to TCBY, where we could sit outside. We go there all the time because they have sorbet for Michelle — she can't have anything with milk in it because she's allergic. But she loves peach sorbet, and Pippa and I love frozen yogurt, so everyone is happy. Buttons sat on my lap while I ate mine and she didn't even try to steal any. Well, only a little, anyway.

If only every mess Buttons made led to ice cream, I thought, maybe I wouldn't mind having such a naughty dog.

Later that night, when Mom came in to say good night to me, I asked her if she thought Buttons would always be a bad dog.

"A bad dog?" Mom said, sounding surprised. She sat down on the bed beside me. "Do you think Buttons is that bad?"

Buttons lifted her head when she heard her name. She *still* refused to sleep on her fancy dog bed. What she really seemed to love was my T-shirts. I had accidentally dropped one on the floor on Tuesday and she immediately grabbed it and rolled on it and then fell asleep on it. I felt bad taking it away from her, since it seemed kind of cute that she liked it. So it was still on the floor, which was totally crazy for me, because I always put everything away immediately. And Buttons was sleeping on it again. Which made me glad, again, that she didn't shed like other dogs.

"Well, she's always digging and running around and making a mess," I said. "It's like she's completely crazy sometimes." I'd lost count of how many baths I'd had to give her already. "I don't understand why she won't lie down and be good."

"She's doing that right now," Mom said.

"Yeah, 'cause it's bedtime," I said.

"That's still pretty great for a puppy," Mom said. "A lot of them cry all night. She's already sleeping very well. You were sweet to give her one of your T-shirts; I bet that makes her feel close to you."

"Oh," I said. I liked that way of looking at it.

"But I think you're onto something," Mom said. "All dogs behave better when they get enough exercise. Maybe we need to tire her out a little more so she'll be calmer when she's home with us."

"How do we do that?" I asked.

"Why don't you take her to the park tomorrow?" Mom said. "I'll get one of your brothers to go with you. You should keep her away from dogs we don't know, but I bet she would really love it."

"OK," I said. I'm not really a "park" person. Danny loves the park that's near us, but he's a ridiculous sports guy, so he likes having all that space to run around and hit baseballs and practice soccer and whatever. When I go to the park, I'm usually like,

OK, now what? I don't want to run around and I'm always worried about getting grass stains on my clothes.

But if it meant tiring Buttons out so she'd be a good dog, I was willing to try it.

It turned out the only brother who was free after school on Thursday was Miguel, and *boy* did he grumble about it. "I don't want to be seen with that furball," "Moooooom, why do I always have to baby-sit," "This is so totally embarrassing," and on and on and *on*.

But Danny had soccer practice and Carlos had a Mathletes meeting and Oliver was taking a practice SAT test, so it had to be Miguel. Which was his own fault anyway, since he doesn't ever do anything except fix his hair and wonder why girls don't talk to him.

He slouched around grumbling while I clipped Buttons' cute pink leash onto her collar.

"I could go by myself," I said. "It's only a few blocks."

"Yeah, right," Miguel said. "I'd be grounded for the next century if I let you go by yourself. But listen, if we see anyone from my class there, you don't know me, OK? And that's definitely not my dog."

I rolled my eyes. "Fine by me!"

I put some plastic bags and a bottle of water and a little plastic bowl in my pink purse, and I changed into my oldest jeans, so that I'd be ready if Buttons decided to climb on me with muddy paws again. Then we started off for the park.

Buttons loved her leash. She kept jumping on it and trying to pin it down with her paws and getting it tangled around her legs. She loved it so much it took her almost two whole blocks to realize that she was outside. Then she had to stop and sniff every blade of grass. A couple of times she tried to stop and roll in the dirt, but I tugged her along so she wouldn't do that.

Miguel walked a few steps ahead of us and pretended we weren't there. Whenever we stopped, he would stop, too, looking around all "la la, just standing here on a street corner, whatever." He pulled out his comb and ran it through his hair a few times, smoothing out the flyaway bits. I don't even remember when Miguel became such a dork. He tried so hard to seem like a macho tough stud for the girls, but I'd never seen any of them talk to him.

When we got to the park, Miguel said, "There's a dog run over this way."

"What's that?" I asked.

"It's a fenced-in area where you can let your dog off the leash," Miguel said. "So she can play with other dogs."

"I don't want her to play with other dogs yet," I said. "Let's just walk and let her sniff things."

Miguel fidgeted and shoved his hands in his pockets. He kept looking around like he was afraid he was being watched. But Buttons was the happiest I'd ever seen her. She ran in big circles on the grass in front of us as we walked. The wind blew a leaf past her nose. With a ferocious yip, she pounced on it, then blinked in surprise when it didn't try to run away. She poked it with her little black nose, then looked up at me like, *Did I win? Did I win?*

And of course she tried to dive under every bush we saw. I could already see tiny green grass stains on her little white paws. Small twigs and leaves hooked in her honey-colored fur as she romped through the park. But I couldn't really get mad at her for it. She was having *such* an amazing time.

As we got closer to the pond in the middle of the park, I heard a loud baying sound. It was so loud and strange that I didn't realize for a minute that it was a dog barking. Buttons knew right away, though. She stood up on her hind legs and lifted her nose in the air, leaning on the end of the leash. With her little front paws folded down, she looked kind of like these meerkats I'd seen on TV.

"AROOOOOF AROOOOOF AROOOOOOF!" went the mystery dog. Then I saw the barker barreling toward us. It was brown and black and white with floppy ears — a beagle, I was pretty sure. A black-and-red leash trailed around its neck. It went "AROOOOOOOOF!" one more time and bounded up to Buttons.

I was about to grab my puppy out of the way when I saw the dog's owner running after her.

"I'm sorry!" she yelled. "That's my dog! She's harmless! Just noisy! I'm sorry!"

I knew who she was — Ella Finegold, the older sister of annoying Isaac. She was in Danny's class at school. Last week she'd done this hilarious awesome song at the talent show with her beagle. So I decided it was OK for Buttons to say hi.

The dog skidded to a stop in front of Buttons and stood there wagging its tail and panting goofily. Buttons sniffed her all over and the dog stayed perfectly still. Then Buttons did the cutest thing. She stood up on her hind legs, put her front paws together, and pawed the air with them, like she was going *Play with me play with me play with me!*

"Trumpet, you wicked thing," Ella said, catching

the beagle's leash. She was panting even more than the dog and her curly brown hair was fluffing out everywhere.

"Hey, I remember you," Miguel said to her. "You won the talent show at Rosie's school."

"I did," Ella said, turning pink. "But mostly it was because of Trumpet." She patted the beagle's side and Trumpet looked up at her with this adoring grin.

"Yeah, it was awesome," Miguel said, letting Trumpet sniff his hand. Buttons flapped her paws madly at Trumpet again.

"Aww, she's so cute," Ella said.

"Ella!" a voice called in the distance. I saw a boy waving from over by the playground. It looked like Nikos Stavros, who's in Danny's class, too. And next to him was a girl I thought might be Rory Mason. Her dad is Danny's baseball coach. She's nice, but she's, like, the total opposite of me — I mean, I guess in a different way than Pippa is. Like, I've never seen Rory without scrapes all over her knees and elbows, and I don't think she'd be caught dead in pink.

"Coming!" Ella called. "See you guys later," she said, and dragged Trumpet away.

Buttons sat down, looking disappointed.

"Don't worry, Buttons," I said. "We'll find you some friends soon."

“That’s a pretty cool dog,” Miguel said, nodding at Ella and Trumpet as they ran off. “Still not big enough, though.”

“Miguel?” said a girl’s voice.

Miguel froze. He’d been so busy saying hi to Trumpet that he’d forgotten to stay away from me and Buttons. And now his worst nightmare had appeared behind us.

Cheerleaders!

CHAPTER 13

I didn't know their names, but I'd seen these two girls outside the high school, sitting under a tree and flipping their hair as the boys went past. I was pretty sure they were cheerleaders.

"Oh. My. Gosh," said the short blond one. She was staring at Buttons.

"Is that your dog?" the tall one with red hair asked Miguel. She pointed at Buttons and tilted her head so the sun caught all the shiny highlights in her hair.

"No," Miguel said quickly. He was totally blushing. "Nuh-uh, nope."

"She is SO. CUTE!" the blond girl squealed. She talked like every other word was its own sentence, with all these dramatic pauses in between. "I just. LOVE HER! I just. Want to spend all day. SNUGGLING HER!"

"Me too!" said the redhead. "Is she yours?" she asked me.

"Uh, she's *ours*," Miguel said quickly. "That's what I meant. Both of ours. Our family's."

Ha. Nice save, Miguel. I could see which way the wind was blowing. "She's really mine," I said.

"Wow, Miguel, you're so sweet to take your little sister and her puppy to the park," said the redhead. She tilted her head again. I was pretty sure she was doing it deliberately to show off her hair in the sunlight. It looked accidental, but she had kind of a faraway expression, like half of her brain was thinking about how she looked all the time.

"Yeah, well, you know, I like to help out," Miguel said.

"Aren't you going to introduce me to your *friends*?" I said to him. He turned even redder.

"This is Caitlin," he said, nodding at the redhead, "and this is Sarah. This is my sister, Rosie."

"Hi," Caitlin said, her gaze drifting back to Buttons. I could tell she was going to forget my name before she even left the park. Definitely not as cool as Miru.

"My parents got us a dog this summer," Sarah said. "But he was SO big and furry and all OVER the place. I was like, YUCK, I mean, PLEASE, couldn't we have a SMALL dog if we have to have anything? You know what I mean?" she said to Miguel, twirling a strand of hair around her finger.

"Yeah, totally!" Miguel said.

"Small dogs are ever so much cuter," Caitlin said, flipping her hair back.

"I know," Miguel said eagerly. "They're way better."

"Miguel has always loved small dogs," I said sweetly. "I said, 'Miguel, don't you want a big tough scary dog?' and he was like, 'No, no, no, we should definitely get something tiny and cute and fuzzy.'"

Miguel shot me a glare.

"Aww, that's adorable," Sarah said, crouching to pat Buttons. Buttons nosed at her hand and she pulled it back quickly. "She doesn't bite, right?"

"Of course not," I said, offended for Buttons. *I* was more likely to bite Sarah than Buttons was.

"So what happened with your dog?" Miguel asked Sarah.

"We gave him to my sister's best friend's little brother," Sarah said. "Like, good luck with that, because he was a total lunatic. He ran away, like, all the time."

Smart dog, I thought.

"So what are you doing here?" I asked. These two

didn't seem like they'd come to the park to play baseball.

"We always come to the park on Thursdays," Caitlin said. "That's when the boys' Ultimate Frisbee practice is."

"We're cheerleaders," Sarah explained. "So we figure we should support them while they're practicing." She exchanged a little smile with Caitlin. I had a feeling if we followed them to the Ultimate playing field, we'd find out that a lot of the boys played with their shirts off.

"That's great," Miguel said. "That's so cool."

"So maybe we'll see you and your puppy next Thursday," Caitlin said to Miguel. Buttons rolled onto her back, and Caitlin gingerly patted her tummy.

"Yeah! Definitely!" Miguel said. "We're always here! Me and my puppy!"

I managed not to laugh, but it was hard.

"We should go," I said to Miguel. "Buttons is getting tired."

"Buttons!" Sarah squealed. "That is SO! ADORABLE!"

"Really?" Miguel said to me. "She doesn't look tired."

Buttons was flopped over in the grass. Her eyes were drooping and her paws twitched like she was already dreaming.

"Miguel," I said firmly.

"OK, 'byeeee," Sarah said.

"'Bye, Miguel," Caitlin said. Her voice made his name sound much more grown-up than when anyone in our house said it.

"See you next Thursday," Miguel said with a huge grin.

The girls sashayed away with their arms linked, giggling. Miguel looked like he'd been run over by a spaceship. His expression was all dazed and silly-looking.

"Come on," I said, grabbing his wrist and dragging him out of the park. Buttons bounced to her paws again as soon as I moved. She found a few more bushes to dive into on our way out. Whenever she spotted the leash out of the corner of her eye, she spun around and pounced on it, which made walking in a straight line kind of difficult, but it was pretty funny.

"They talked to me," Miguel said in a wondering voice when we were a block away from the park. "Did you see that? That really happened, didn't it? Caitlin and Sarah talked to me!"

"I guess you could call that talking," I said. "Mostly they flipped their hair at you."

"They've never talked to me before," Miguel said. "I can't believe they know my name. How's my hair? Does it look OK?"

"They didn't care about *your* hair," I said. "They just wanted you to notice *their* hair."

"They have great hair," Miguel said dreamily.

"I forbid you to date those girls, Miguel. They're total dimwits."

"They *loved* Buttons," Miguel said. The puppy looked up at him with her tongue hanging out of the side of her mouth. She wagged her tail and he bent down to ruffle her fur. "You're the best dog ever," he said.

Wow! "'Best dog ever?'" I said. "What happened to 'too small, too fuzzy, too embarrassing'?"

"Well," Miguel said loftily, "if I had *known* that girls liked *little* dogs I would have voted *differently* from the beginning, wouldn't I?"

"Um, I'm a girl," I said. "That didn't tip you off?"

"Yeah, but you're Rosie," he said.

That was true. And I was very glad to be Rosie, and not Sarah or Caitlin, thank you very much. Even if they did have great hair.

On the plus side, Miguel's newfound love for Buttons meant that it was easy to convince him to give her a bath when we got home. I supervised, but he was the one who got all wet, which was very satisfying. Then we dried her off and took her into the living room. She rolled around madly on the couch, sprinting from one end to the other and nose-diving into the cushions with happy *rrrrrruffs*. Miguel sat on the arm of the couch and laughed.

"What *are* you doing?" Danny asked, poking his head into the room.

"Playing with Buttons," I said.

"Isn't she hilarious?" Miguel said.

"Miguel!" Danny said, sounding shocked. "Don't tell me you've gone over to the dark side, too."

"Hey!" I said.

"Well, she *is* cute," Miguel said with a shrug.

Danny buried his head in his hands. "This is terrible," he said. "I thought I could count on you guys!" He pointed at Buttons. "That is not a real dog. Merlin is a real dog. Real dogs are big and chase tennis balls. One day I'm going to get a real dog, and until I do, I want nothing to do with that fluffhead."

"Good!" I shouted after him as he stomped away. "You leave her alone! She's too good for you anyway!"

"He'll come around," Miguel said. "OK, I have to go e-mail my friends. Caitlin and Sarah! Craziness!" He left the room, shaking his head.

Buttons flopped over with her head on my lap.

"Boys are ridiculous, Buttons," I said, scratching her belly.

Snnzzzzzzrt, she agreed. And in half a minute, she was asleep.

When Dad got home from work, he found us on the couch. I was reading, and Buttons had rolled sideways so she was asleep with all four paws in the air. Dad grinned, putting his briefcase down by the door.

"Shh," I said. "It totally worked. We took her to the park and now she's all tuckered out."

"Aww," Dad said. "What a good dog. Have your brothers been playing with her?"

"They all like her now," I said. "Except Danny. And I don't care, because he's lame anyway."

"Great," Dad said. "Want to make some peppermint meringue cookies?"

He remembered! My dad was so busy, I always expected him to forget stuff like that. But he had brought home all the ingredients we needed and everything. Buttons stayed asleep on the couch while I went to the kitchen with Dad. Later I saw Oliver in there patting her. He looked all mopey again, but when she batted at his hand he laughed.

The cookies came out totally perfect. Dad separated the eggs for me, but he let me hold the electric beater to make the meringue all fluffy and peaked. We put pretty pink and purple glittery sprinkles on top of them, and in the end it was the prettiest batch of cookies I'd ever seen. Of course, then I had to keep a close eye on the kitchen all night to make sure none of my brothers snuck in and ate them.

"Hey!" I yelled when I caught Danny peeking under the foil.

"Can't I have one?" he said. "Just one?"

"No, you can't, poodle-hater," I said. "Not unless you bring twenty-five cents to school tomorrow and buy one like everyone else."

"Bossyboots," he grumbled, wandering back out to the den.

"The Africans will thank you when their goat arrives!" I called cheerfully after him.

Buttons was calm and sleepy for the rest of the evening. When we let her out, she trotted into the yard and then came right back in with no digging at all. She slept on my feet while I did my homework. At one point her paws started twitching and she made these cute tiny yips in her sleep, as if she was dreaming about racing around the park with Trumpet.

When I went to bed, I tried putting my T-shirt in the dog bed and tucking Buttons in there. I don't know if she was just too tired to climb out, but she curled right up and went to sleep. In her bed! Finally!

"See?" I said. "Why couldn't you do that from the start?"

I was happy that Buttons was so sweet and good after her trip to the park. But I was worried, too. I couldn't take her to the park every day. I had the bake sale tomorrow after school. There would be a lot more homework later in the school year. And I wanted to try out for the school play this year, which would mean lots of rehearsals. How was I going to make sure Buttons got enough exercise to be a good dog all the time?

CHAPTER 14

"That will be seventy-five cents," I said to Heidi Tyler. She had three different kinds of cookies in her hand and there were already crumbs all over her shirt.

"Oh, man, how did I do that?" Heidi said, trying to brush them off and getting more crumbs in her hair. "Here you go, Rosie." She handed me a five-dollar bill and I gave her four dollars and a quarter in change.

"You do that so fast," said Charlie Grayson. "I have to think about it for half an hour." Charlie is the shortest boy in our class. He's really quiet, like Danny's friend Eric, who I mentioned earlier, so I was glad he was at my table for the bake sale. He let me handle all the money, which was totally fun. And he didn't tell on me when I "accidentally" broke one of the cookies — maybe because I let him have the other half.

Our table was at the front door of the school. Pippa and Arnold Scott were at a table at the back door, so we could be sure to get everyone going in and out at the end of the day. And Michelle and Kerri Drake were standing at the entrance to the parking lot with a big sign, so parents would have their money ready by the time they got to the doors.

We sold half our stuff during lunch and everything else was nearly gone only fifteen minutes after school ended. But there was still one peppermint meringue cookie left when Eric Lee came by the table, and he bought it, which confirmed my opinion that Eric is cooler than your average sixth-grade boy. He was all quiet and mumbly about it, too, which I thought was cute.

At one point while I was counting our change, I sensed someone sneaking up behind me. I whipped around and grabbed Isaac's wrist right before he pulled off my ribbon.

"Isaac, *stop it*!" I snapped. "Why are you SUCH A BRAT?"

"I didn't DO anything!" he protested, yanking on his arm.

"Well, buy a cookie or go away!" I said.

He bought a cookie and *then* went away, which was the best of both worlds.

A pair of little brown eyes peeked over the top of the table. I leaned forward and saw that it was Eden, Troy's little sister. She had this huge smile on her face, like always. Next to her was another second-grade girl who looked familiar, but I wasn't sure who she was. She had straight black hair in two pigtails and glasses with blue frames.

"Can-I have-a cookie-for me-and one-for Yun-too?" Eden said in a sweet singsong voice. She reached up and put two quarters on the table.

"Sure," I said. "Do you want peanut butter or chocolate chip or chocolate chocolate chip?"

Eden looked thoughtful. This was clearly a very important decision.

"Peanut butter," said Yun. She looked behind her at a car that was pulling into one of the parking spots. "OK?" she called. "Peanut butter OK?"

I was totally excited when I saw that it was Miru driving the car. I realized Yun must be her little sister. She parked and came over to us, swinging her keys around her fingers, all cool-like. I'm going to swing my keys like that when I can drive.

"Sure," she said. "I'll have one, too. Hi, Rosie."

"Hey, Miru," I said, taking her quarter and trying to act as if I hang out with high schoolers all the time. Charlie looked all wide-eyed and amazed that I knew a high schooler, especially one as cool as Miru. "Last two," I said, giving one to Yun and one to Miru.

"Chocolate chocolate chip," Eden burst out.

"Good choice," I said, handing her the cookie in a napkin. Her smile got even bigger and she ran off to join Troy and Parker in the playground.

"Looks like you're almost done," Miru said, nodding at the empty plates on the table.

"I know!" I said. "I thought I was going to be here until four at least! Mom's not supposed to pick me up until then, when she's done at the store."

"Want a ride home?" Miru asked.

Did I! A ride in Miru's car! Holy cow! "Yeah, OK," I said with a shrug.

"I'll call your mom and make sure it's all right," Miru said, pulling out her cell phone. "Come on, Yun, let's wait for Rosie to sell the rest of her cookies."

"We could help," Yun said through a mouthful of cookie. "We could eat dem all."

Miru laughed and took her sister over to the steps.

"She's my brother's girlfriend," I said to Charlie. "We're, like, practically best friends."

"Wow," he said. "My big brother barely even speaks to me. He won't let me anywhere near his friends."

"Oh," I said. That sounded sad. I didn't know Charlie had a big brother.

When we finally sold all the cookies, Ms. Applebaum took the money box and told us we did a great job. She said she'd put away the table and everything, so I could go home. The coolest part is that Miru let me sit in the front seat, and Yun didn't mind or anything. I *never* get to sit in the front seat in my parents' car.

"Are you coming in to see Oliver?" I asked Miru as we pulled out of the school parking lot.

She snorted. "I'm sure he doesn't want me to."

"Uh, I'm sure he *does*," I said.

"Yeah, right," she said. "He doesn't care about anything except college applications. I want a guy who can be sensitive and emotional, Rosie. Like, you know what happened on Sunday?"

I remembered Oliver coming home early from their bike ride. "You were busy?" I guessed.

"Ha!" she said. "I'll tell you what happened. We got to my house and I was like, 'OK, awesome, what should we do now?' and he was like, 'I don't know, what do you want to do?' and I said, 'I don't know, what do you want to do?' and he was like, 'Wow, man, I'm totally freaking out about college applications, aren't you?' and I was like, 'Wait, so, you want to go home and work on them?' and he was like, 'Oh, I don't know, do you?' and I was like, 'Dude, if that's what *you* want, then fine, I have stuff to do anyway,' and *he* was like, 'Oh, well, I guess if you have stuff to do . . .' and I was like 'Yeah, I totally do, 'bye then,' and he was like, 'OK, 'bye then,' CAN YOU BELIEVE THAT?"

"Um," I said. "Believe what?"

"That he did that! I'm telling you, Rosie, hold out for a good guy. Make him tell you he likes you up front so it's not all confusing and lame."

Well, she was right about one thing. I was really confused. "Oliver does like you," I said. That was the one thing I was pretty sure of.

"He never acts like it!" Miru said. "He's all closed off and quiet and whatever."

Oliver was totally not quiet, at least not around my other brothers.

"I just wish he cared about anything," Miru said.

Right then I had a brilliant idea. And this one was really brilliant, not paint-my-dog's-nails-pink brilliant.

"I want to show you something," I said. "At my house. Really quickly. OK?"

We pulled into my driveway. Miru didn't ask a bunch of questions. She just turned off the car, told Yun to stay there, and followed me over to the window that looks into the living room.

Sure enough, Oliver was in there, playing with Buttons. They were both lying on the carpet, facing each other. Oliver made his hands sneak up on Buttons. She would be watching one intently, and then the other would creep up on her other side. So she'd spin around and then the other hand would make a break for it. He swept his hand under her paws and she went *RRRRRR!* and pounced on it. But he was too fast for her, so she chased it all around the carpet, going "Rrrrr! Yip! Rrrrr!"

Finally she caught the cuff of his long-sleeve shirt in her teeth. With a triumphant *snrrft!* she started backing up, trying to drag his hand along behind her.

Oliver started laughing so hard he had to roll onto his back. Of course, Buttons instantly dropped the sleeve and sprang onto his chest. She braced herself on his shoulders and stretched down to lick his nose. Oliver put up his hands to stop her and she happily licked his hands instead. Then she sat down on his chest with this pleased look like she had just found Antarctica and claimed it for the Kingdom of Buttons.

"Whoa," Miru whispered.

"Cute, right?" I said. For a moment I was worried. If she didn't think it was cute, this could be the end of Oliver and Miru, and it would be my fault. But how could she look at him with Buttons and think he didn't care about anything? Oliver was a big softie, that was the truth.

Miru smiled at me. "Yeah, OK," she said. "Pretty cute."

"Maybe he's not so bad?" I tried.

"Maybe I'll just say hi for a minute," she said.

We got Yun from the car and went inside. Oliver sat up when we walked in. His hair was all messed up from rolling around on the carpet. He looked really surprised to see Miru.

"Oh!" he said. "Hi! I — um — I didn't think —"

"Come here, you," Miru said, taking his hand and disappearing into the den with him.

Buttons bounded over and tried to climb my leg. I picked her up and let Yun pet her. "Want to see if there are any extra meringue cookies hiding in the kitchen?" I said to her.

"Yes!" she said, nodding so her pigtails bounced around.

Yun ate her cookie while I practiced Buttons' tricks using dog treats. I let Yun give her a treat, too. Buttons delicately licked it out of her hand and then wagged her tail, giving Yun big moon eyes like Yun was her new best friend ever. Yun giggled a lot when that happened.

Miru didn't stay for long, but Oliver looked much, *much* happier after she left. He even came outside to run around the yard with me and Buttons, which really meant *he* ran around the yard with her (while she barked and barked with joy) and I watched, because I don't like to run, but it was perfect because it tired her out.

And then he called Buttons the "best dog ever," too.

"Look at that," I said to her at bedtime. "I think my brothers like you even more than they like me." She jumped into her bed and smiled up at me, panting. Then she went *dig dig dig dig dig* until my T-shirt was exactly the way she wanted it, and then she conked out.

I was happy, though. I felt like I had helped Oliver and Miru in a good way. Now maybe Oliver wouldn't be so mopey anymore. That should make up for all the times he let me use his computer. Right?

And it wasn't just me. Buttons had helped, too.

For such a bad dog, sometimes she did remarkably good things . . . even if she didn't know she was doing them.

"Good night, Buttons," I whispered.

Snzzzzzzzzrt, she replied.

CHAPTER 15

Buttons woke me Saturday morning by trying to lick off my ear.

"Eurgh!" I yelped, fending her off. "Buttons, how did you get up here?" Then I saw my mom sitting on the bed with us.

"Morning, *chiquita*," Mom said. "I'm making pancakes, and then your dad would love to go to the park with you and Buttons."

"Puppy, pancakes, and park!" I said, fluffing Buttons' fur around her face. She flopped over on her back and I threw the sheets over her.

RRRRRRrrrrrARRRRrrraaarrrr! Buttons yammered, rolling around and wrestling with the covers. I pulled the sheets back again and she lay there with her paws in the air, her black eyes sparkling mischievously at me. I rubbed her tummy. She wriggled to her paws and bounced over to bury herself in my pillows.

“Five minutes to pancakes!” Mom said, and left the room.

I got dressed quickly and carried Buttons downstairs. I don’t know if she could tell that I was excited, but she seemed excited, too. She scrambled up to my shoulder, grabbed my pink hair ribbon in her teeth, and shook it with a little *rrrrrrrft!*

“Buttons, leave it alone,” I said, rescuing my ribbon and putting Buttons down on the living room floor. Dad was setting the table for pancakes. He grinned when he saw me.

“Would you mind some company today?” he asked. “I want to play with this famous dog, too.”

“Sure!” I said. The best thing about doing stuff with Dad is that he usually buys me ice cream on our way home, even if it’s nearly dinnertime. So I can’t imagine ever saying no to him. Plus maybe I could get him to give Buttons her bath when we got home!

Only Miguel and Carlos were there for breakfast. Oliver was already out with Miru, and Danny apparently left early to go hang out with Parker — and, of course, Merlin. Dad asked my brothers if they wanted to come with us, but Miguel had friends coming over to play video games, and Mom wanted Carlos to help her with a computer problem.

So it was just me and Dad and Buttons walking to the park. Dad laughed and laughed when he saw the way Buttons wrestled with her leash. "She's a character, isn't she?" he said, which was funny because I've heard him say the same thing about me.

At the park we decided to try the dog run. I hadn't been in there before, but it was empty when we got there, and it was *huge*. There were grassy bits and pebbly bits and wood chip bits and a fountain in the middle that you could turn on with your foot.

"Can I let her off the leash?" I asked Dad.

"It looks all fenced in," Dad said, glancing around. "Sure, let's try it."

I unclipped the sparkly pink leash from Buttons' collar and put it in my purse. She sat down and tilted her head at me.

"Go on, run around," I said, waving at her.

She tilted her head the other way.

"Hey, Buttons!" Dad cried. "Can't catch me!" And he took off running to the other end of the dog run.

Buttons jumped to her paws when he moved. She looked really startled. It took her a minute to realize where he'd gone, and then she went tearing after him, going *Rrrft! Rrrft! Rrrrrrrft!* like she was yelling, *Don't you dare! I'm going to get you!*

She was nearly as fast as Dad, but the funniest

thing is that she was clever, so she kept cutting him off when he went around things or scooting under benches and pouncing on his feet when he paused to look for her.

They were running back toward me when something flew through the air and landed in the dog run. Buttons stopped dead and stared at it as it bounced and rolled into the fountain. She decided to abandon Dad and run over to investigate.

Dad and I caught up to her as she was pawing at her new treasure, which turned out to be a tennis ball. An old, ripped-up tennis ball that looked like it had been seriously drooled on.

"Lucky Buttons!" Dad said. He reached for it, but Buttons jumped in, managed to get her whole tiny mouth around it, and trotted away. She sat down about ten feet away and gave Dad a look like, *Don't even try it, buster. I found it! It's mine!* She put the ball down between her front paws and sniffed it all over.

We heard the gate of the dog run opening behind us, and when we turned around, we saw that it was Danny, Parker, Troy, and Eric. And charging into the dog run ahead of them was perfect Mr. Merlin himself.

"Oh, *no*," Danny yelled, spotting us. But the other guys were already waving.

"Hi, Rosie! Hi, Mr. Sanchez!" they called.

Merlin didn't bother saying hi. He rocketed right past us and shot over to Buttons. For a moment I was afraid he'd run right over her without noticing she was there, but he stopped when he was nose-to-nose with her. His tail was waving so hard I could practically feel the breeze from where I was.

Buttons bounced to her paws and trotted around him in a circle, sniffing any part of him she could reach. Merlin stood still with his tail wagging, letting her examine him. He sort of twisted his head back over his shoulder to look at us, as if he was hoping we could explain what the small fluffy thing was doing to him.

"Come on, guys, let's go," Danny said to his friends, backing away from us.

"Wait — is that your dog?" Parker asked me.

"Yup," I said. "That's Buttons!"

"You didn't tell us you got a dog," Eric said to Danny.

"You *didn't*?" I said. "Danny!"

"Well, she's not a real dog!" Danny said. "I mean, look at her. She's just a furball. How are you supposed to play with a dog like that? She's for Rosie, anyway."

"That's not true," Dad said. "She's supposed to be for all of you."

"Yeah. Everyone *else* likes her," I said.

"Including Merlin, apparently," Parker joked. Merlin had dropped into a play bow with his butt up in the air and his tail going like mad. Buttons stepped back and looked at him for a moment, then bounced forward like she was going to pounce on his nose.

"RRUFF! RRUFF!" Merlin barked, spinning in a circle.

And then suddenly they were running. They didn't even seem to know who was chasing who. Merlin dashed in one direction with Buttons right on his tail, and then Buttons came flying back the other way with Merlin right behind her. She did the same tricks she'd pulled on Dad, where she'd suddenly dart under a bench, and then Merlin kind of spun around looking confused, and then she'd pop out again and take off at a million miles an hour, and he'd bark with excitement and go pelting after her.

"Um, Danny?" Parker said. "I hate to be the one to tell you this, but your dog is supercute."

"I *know* she's cute," Danny said. "That's exactly the *problem*."

"Dude, I don't know what you're complaining about," Troy said. "At least you have a dog. At least she'll run around outside with you."

"Yeah," Eric said. "Try living with two cats who hate you, and then tell me your life is tough."

"This is so awesome," Parker said, watching the dogs roll around together. "I've been hoping we could find another dog for Merlin to play with. Man, he totally loves her!"

"But she's not the kind of dog who *really* plays," Danny said. "I mean, look at this." He went over and grabbed the tennis ball that Buttons had dropped. "Hey, dogs!" he called.

Merlin and Buttons both stopped running and turned to look at him. Danny threw the tennis ball so it flew all the way to the other end of the dog run.

Both dogs took off after it. Merlin had longer legs, so he got there first. He picked up the tennis ball in his mouth.

"See?" Danny said. "Like a real dog should."

Merlin lay down and started to chew on the tennis ball.

"Merlin! No!" Parker called. "Quit eating the tennis ball! Bring it back here! Merlin, bring the ball!"

Merlin's ears scooted forward and he raised his head to look at Parker. His tail thumped on the grass. Then he went back to chewing on the ball.

"We're still working on the 'fetching' part of 'fetch,'" Parker said sheepishly to me and Dad.

Buttons finally caught up to Merlin. She ran right up to his front paws and poked his nose with her nose. Surprised, Merlin sat up. Buttons grabbed the tennis ball in her mouth and trotted away with it. Her tail and nose were held high, like she was rather proud of herself.

"Hey!" Danny said. "She stole his ball!"

"That's OK, I brought more," Parker said. "She can have it if she wants."

Buttons trotted all the way back down the dog run to us and dropped the ball at Danny's feet. Then she sat down and looked up at him with a pleased expression on her face.

"What?" Danny said to her.

"I think she wants you to throw it again," Troy said.

"Yeah, whatever," Danny said, crossing his arms. Buttons tilted her head to the side, and then pawed at his sneaker.

"Aw, come on, Danny, throw the ball for her," Parker said.

"How can you say no to that face?" Troy asked.

I looked over at Dad and he grinned at me. I wanted to jump in and take the ball and throw it myself, but finally Danny bent down and picked it up.

"She doesn't really know what she's doing," he said. "I bet she won't do it again." He tossed the tennis ball just a little distance away. Immediately Buttons sprinted over and grabbed it. Again she came trotting back and dropped it at Danny's feet.

"Holy cow," Parker said. "She can fetch! She fetches way better than Merlin!" At the other end of the dog run, Merlin was rolling gleefully in a pile of leaves.

"And she's only a puppy," I said proudly.

"It's instinctive," Dad said. "Some dogs are natural fetchers."

Danny didn't say anything. He just kind of looked at Buttons for a while. She wagged her tail at him. Actually, because she was so excited, it was more like she wagged her whole butt.

"Well, I think you're lucky," Troy said to Danny. "I'd rather have a silly-looking dog than no dog at all."

"Totally," Eric said.

Which wasn't exactly the ringing praise I thought Buttons deserved, but it was still better than Danny's grumbling and refusing to play with her.

Finally Danny picked up the ball and threw it again, farther this time. Buttons shot after it like she had to catch it in order to save the world. She pounced on it as it rolled and it shot out from between her paws. Yipping indignantly, she chased after it and pinned it down, then brought it back in triumph.

"Merlin!" Parker called. "Come on, boy! You can do this, too! Maybe Buttons will set a good example for him."

Merlin thought about it for a long time and eventually decided to come back and grace us with his presence. Parker took out another tennis ball, let him sniff it, and threw it for him in the opposite direction from Buttons' ball.

Merlin started to lope toward it, but Buttons apparently decided Danny wasn't throwing fast enough, because she dropped her ball at Danny's feet, raced past Merlin and grabbed his ball, too.

The big golden dog poked his nose at her like he was thinking about trying to get it back, but Buttons jumped away, stuck her tail in his face, and came galloping back to us.

"Wow. She's just like Rosie," Parker said.

"Just like me?" I said. "What?"

"Look at her bossing Merlin around," Parker said, laughing. "It's just like you and Danny."

"I don't—" I started to say, but then Buttons bounced at Merlin's head again. The bigger dog jumped back with a goofy startled face and it made me laugh.

"Plus you can tell everyone's going to spoil her rotten," Danny said. "Just like they spoil Rosie."

"THEY DO NOT," I said.

"Another bossy little princess in your house," Troy said. "That's totally hilarious."

"Yeah," Danny said. "I guess it's kind of funny."

When Danny wasn't looking, Dad gave me a fist bump and a wink.

I wasn't sure how I felt about it, though. I liked the idea that Buttons and I had something in common. And I guess it was a good thing if my brothers all liked her. I watched Danny throwing the tennis ball for Buttons and it made me think that it would be easier to keep her happy and well-behaved if all my brothers helped. But what if she liked them more than she liked me? What if they took her away from me?

Still, what Parker and Danny said made me feel kind of warm and glowy inside. Maybe Buttons was more like me than I'd thought. Maybe she really *was* my dog . . . even if my brothers liked her, too.

CHAPTER 16

We played with Buttons for almost an hour and by then she was definitely getting tired. The last time Danny threw the tennis ball, she started to chase it, but halfway there she flopped down on the grass and stretched out with her nose between her front paws. Merlin went over to sniff her and she batted playfully at his nose without getting up.

"We should let the puppy get some rest," Dad said. "Ready to go home, Rosie?"

"Yeah, OK," I said. We left the boys there with Merlin. I noticed that Danny patted Buttons' head as she trotted past him. And so did Eric, which just confirmed all my plans for him, too.

I ended up carrying Buttons most of the way home. She went all floppy in my arms and rested her head and front paws on my shoulder. I could hear her little *snzzzzrr*ing noises near my ear. Her fluffy fur was soft and warm under my hands, and I didn't even mind that there were twigs and bits of grass caught in it.

"You know what's funny?" Dad said. "I was thinking about what the guys said back there. The truth is, when we brought you home as a baby, all the boys had the same reaction to you that they did to Buttons — like, 'What is that small fluffy creature? A sister! She's going to be no fun at all. No, thank you.' But then they each warmed up to you, just like they did to Buttons. You clearly turned out to be a whole lot of fun. And now, of course, they all like you the way you are."

They did?

I snuggled Buttons closer to me. "Not as much as they like Buttons, though," I said.

Dad tugged on my ponytail. "Well, who do you like better?" he said. "Buttons or them?"

I laughed. "Buttons, definitely."

Mom let me sleep in on Sunday. She snuck into my room and got Buttons so the puppy wouldn't wake me up. I didn't sleep very late, but when I came downstairs, I found Carlos in the kitchen trying to teach Buttons to roll over. She seemed pretty confused. He could get her onto her back but then she kind of lay there with her ears flopped back and blinked at him like, *Is this what you want?*

"Goofy dog," Carlos said to her. "Keep rolling!"

She wriggled around so her head was tilting the other way at him.

"OK, good try," he said, letting her have the treat. "I think I'm doing something wrong. Maybe I should check the Internet for tips." Which was hilarious, because normally Carlos thinks he's doing everything right and it's the rest of us getting it wrong.

I poured myself a bowl of cereal and sat on a stool by the island, next to Oliver. He also had a bowl of cereal in front of him, but he was just kind of staring into space with a loopy smile. I could tell he'd been doing that for a while because his cereal was all soggy.

I waved my spoon in front of his face and he jumped.

"Oh, hey," he said. "Oh, Rosie!"

"Yeah, that's me," I said.

"I was thinking," he said. "Do you and Buttons want to go for a walk with me and Miru today?"

I stared at him. "Seriously? Me?"

"No, wait!" Miguel yelled, popping into the kitchen from the den. "She can't! They have to come to the cheerleaders' car wash with me!"

"We do?" I said.

"Come on, Rosie," Miguel pleaded. "If we show

up with Buttons, I bet Caitlin and Sarah will talk to me again. Maybe Emma will, too!"

"But you don't have a car," I pointed out. "Or, you know, a license."

"Yeah, and besides, I want to go to the park with Rosie and Buttons today," Carlos said.

I nearly fell off my stool. This had never happened to me before in my entire life. "Are you guys making fun of me?" I asked.

"Uh, no," Carlos said, like *I* was the one being weird. "I want to see if Buttons will chase things or catch them in the air or any of that stuff."

"She will," Danny said, clattering down the stairs. "She's great at it. Rosie, I'm going to hang out with Parker and Merlin again today. Want to come?"

"Stop, stop, stop," Oliver said in his Mr. Reasonable voice. "I asked her first. Rosie and Buttons are hanging out with me and Miru."

"But they can do that any day!" Miguel said. "The cheerleaders' car wash is only today!"

"Didn't you already say you get Rosie and Buttons every Thursday?" Carlos pointed out. "That sounds like enough cheerleader time to me."

"Yeah, well, *you* said you were going to go to an obedience class with them," Danny said. "So I think *I* should get to hang out with them on the weekends, when Parker and Merlin are free."

My brothers all started arguing at once. I couldn't believe it.

They were fighting over *me*. They all wanted to hang out with *me*! Well, me and Buttons. But we came together. We were a pair. That's how my brothers saw us. They wanted both of us. I didn't even care who won, because I was winning most of all.

Buttons came over and poked my foot with her nose. I picked her up and she snuggled into me, licking my chin. I realized I really didn't care if she got muddy sometimes or knocked things over or made a mess. She was still my dog.

"You know what, Buttons?" I whispered to her. "You're not so bad after all."

She wagged her tail and went "Rrrruff!" . . . as if she were saying, *Yeah, I know.*

Meatball is a great dog . . .
when he isn't getting into trouble!

Pet Trouble

Bulldog Won't Budge

Turn the page for a sneak peek!

I pressed my nose to the glass door, squinting through the rain.

There was a bulldog sitting right outside. He was staring in at me just like I was staring out at him.

I've never seen a glummer face. I mean, I think that's kind of a funny word — glum — but that was the first thought that popped into my head when I saw this dog's face. He wasn't just sad. He wasn't gloomy. He was definitely glum.

His little dark brown ears drooped. His big, broad shoulders drooped. His long, floppy jowls drooped. His forehead was wrinkled in a worried way, and his sad brown eyes seemed to be saying, *Why am I so wet? And so alone? And so abandoned? And so very, very wet?*

For a moment I thought he was just hanging out on the sidewalk for no reason. But then I realized that he was wearing a red leash — and the leash was tied to the vestibule's front door.

I thought I should run back and get my mom. But I didn't want to leave him in the pouring rain even one second longer. I pulled open the inner door and yelled, "MOM!" really loud. Then I let it close and went to push open the outer door.

The bulldog sat up a little straighter, looking at me hopefully. The brown-and-white fur on his neck stood up in little wet spikes. I untangled his leash from the door handle, which was sort of tough because it was pretty wet and slippery. I had to stand in the rain and get totally drenched. But I got it free and then I held the door open and beckoned to the dog.

"Come on, boy," I said.

He didn't need any more encouragement than that. He rocketed inside so quickly, he nearly bowled me over. He stood inside our vestibule and shook and shook himself. His jowls went *flap-flap-flap-flap-flap*. He sprayed me all over with water, but it didn't matter because I was already wet. My sneakers went *squeak-squish-squeak-squish* as I tried to wring out my shirt without taking it off.

The bulldog's wheezing and snorting echoed around the vestibule. He looked up at me with big trusting eyes — that's the kind of look my mom gets from the sweetest dogs when they're like, *maybe if I look really pathetic you'll put away that needle.* Like he was afraid I would leave and he was hoping if he looked really woebegone I'd stay with him.

I realized that there was a piece of paper folded and tucked into his collar, under his chin. I crouched down to reach for it, and the dog came over and butted my hand with his head. I scratched behind his ears and under his broad chin until I could reach the note, and then I pulled it out. But when I stopped petting the dog, he plowed into my knees and I fell back on my butt. This was apparently exactly what he hoped would happen. He immediately tried to climb into my lap and lick my chin.

Danny's dog, Buttons, had done the same thing at the park on Sunday, but Buttons is a puppy the size of a baseball and she weighs about as much as one. This was a full-grown bulldog, and he was *heavy*. I swear he felt like he weighed as much as me. His big white paws planted themselves on my chest and his enormous pink tongue went *sluuuuuuuurrrrrp!* up the side of my face like a giant piece of wet sandpaper.

I tried to push him off, but he was really, really determined to show me how glad he was to be in out of the rain. He was like, *I must pin you down and say thank you by licking off your face! How else will you know how grateful I am?!* I could feel his tiny stub of a tail wagging up the whole length of his wet, roly-poly body.

"OK!" I cried as he licked me again. "I get it! You're welcome!"

The inside door opened. "Eric?" my mom said as she came out. "Did you — oh my goodness!" Her mouth fell open. She stared at the bulldog, who was flopped across my chest. He looked up at her with a panting, slobbering grin. His tongue was as wide as my hand and it flapped up and down as he breathed, *FLAP HUFF FLAP HUFF FLAP HUFF.*

"Where — what —" My mom pointed at the bulldog. "Eric!"

"He was sitting outside," I said. "In the rain, Mom! Someone left him tied to the front door."

"Tied to the front door?" Mom sounded indignant now.

"In the *rain*," I said again.

I saw Parker and Mr. Green crowd up behind her. Merlin poked his nose through the gap between their legs. His eyes lit up when he saw the bulldog, but Parker held on to him so he couldn't rush forward and say hi.

"There's a note," I said, holding it out so Mom could rescue it from me. I needed my other hand to fend off the slobbermeister.

"Check his tags," she said as she unfolded it. I wrestled the dog's giant head aside so I could see the plain black collar hidden in the folds of his neck. There was only one tag hanging from it, a silver one shaped like a dog bone. And all it said was "Meatball."

"Meatball?" I said to him. He buried his whole wet face in my neck and went *snorftle snorftle*, so I guess that was a yes.

"Please take care of Meatball," my mom read out loud. The paper was soggy and falling apart in her hands. "We cannot have him anymore. Thank you." She threw her hands up. "Of course it isn't signed! They're lucky I can't find them and tell them what I think of them. This poor dog. I'm sure they just thought he was an adorable puppy and had no idea how big he would get."

"Or how loud," I said as Meatball went *SNOOOOOORRRRRG* right in my ear.

"Why would they bring him here instead of an animal shelter?" Mr. Green asked. "Do you know him?"

Mom shook her head. "I've never seen him before. I haven't had any bulldogs in here this year. I wouldn't be surprised if they drove over from another town. One of my colleagues online told me about a dog left at her office, too — like they figure a vet must know how to take care of it."

"And they guess a vet would want to," Parker pointed out.

I'd finally managed to sit up, but Meatball had planted himself firmly in my lap and was snuffling up and down my chest with his big squashed-up nose.

His forehead was wrinkled forward over his serious brown eyes. He shoved his head inside my jacket. I scratched the folds of wrinkles around his neck. Meatball was absolutely soaked. I wondered how long he'd been sitting outside.

"Let's bring him inside and scan him for a microchip," Mom said.

"A microchip?" Parker said with a grin. "You mean he might be a robot dog?"

"Yeah, right," I said. "No one would make a robot dog this slobbery."

Mom grabbed Meatball's collar and wrestled him off me. Finally we got him onto the metal table and he immediately lay down and flopped over with his head as close to me as he could get it. I rubbed his solid white belly while Mom looked for a microchip.

"Of course not," she muttered. "Does nobody want you, poor boy?" She tugged on one of his floppy ears. Meatball rolled onto his stomach, wiggled toward me, and pawed at my jacket, which by this point was covered in little wet brown-and-white dog hairs.

"Oh, I'm an idiot," I said, realizing why he loved my jacket so much. I pulled out one of the dog biscuits I'd found in the waiting room. "Is this what you're looking for?" I said, offering it to him.

SNORF. The biscuit disappeared in a whoosh

of crunching and slurping. Meatball licked the palm of my hand a few times for good measure, leaving it damp and sticky.

"I'll call Wags to Whiskers and see if they have room for him tonight," Mom said.

"Wait," I said. "Can't we take him home with us? Look how much he likes us."

Meatball helpfully rolled over and gave her a winning upside-down grin.

Mom gave Mr. Green one of those grown-up looks. Parker's dad shrugged. "I'd have trouble saying no to either of those faces," he said, nodding at me and Meatball.

"One night," Mom said with a sigh. "And I'll check him over first. Eric, call your sisters and tell them we'll be late for dinner."

Parker followed me out to the waiting room and high-fived me. "Maybe this is it," he said. "Maybe you finally have a dog!"

I hadn't really thought about *keeping* Meatball, like, *forever* and ever. He wasn't exactly the dog I'd always pictured for myself.

But I couldn't send him off to a shelter all by himself. Poor guy. I just wanted to give him somewhere warm and friendly to go. Did that mean we had to keep him? Was I stuck with him now?

Have you gotten

Runaway Retriever

Merlin is a great dog. Parker's new golden retriever is a guy's best friend, with tons of energy for walks and playing catch. And Merlin clearly thinks Parker is the best thing since rawhide bones.

There's just one thing . . .

Merlin is an escape artist. No fence is too high, no cage too strong to keep him from following Parker everywhere he goes. Can Parker make Merlin sit—and *stay*?

For more great dog stories, be sure to check out: